```
F                      01-2065
Sco     Scott, Cynthia
        Built to last
```

DISCARD

DATE DUE			
MR 2 0 '02			
MY 19 '04			
AUG 2 9 2007			
APR 0 2 2008			
JUL 1 5 2009			
SEP 1 5 2010			
MAR 0 9 2011			
SEP 2 6 2012			

SOMERSWORTH PUBLIC LIBRARY
25 MAIN STREET
SOMERSWORTH, NH 03878-3198 GAYLORD M2

BUILT TO LAST

BUILT TO LAST

•

Cynthia Scott

AVALON BOOKS
NEW YORK

© Copyright 2002 by Cynthia Scott
Library of Congress Catalog Card Number: 2001097168
ISBN 0-8034-9514-5
All rights reserved.
All the characters in this book are fictitious,
and any resemblance to actual persons,
living or dead, is purely coincidental.
Published by Thomas Bouregy & Co., Inc.
160 Madison Avenue, New York, NY 10016

PRINTED IN THE UNITED STATES OF AMERICA
ON ACID-FREE PAPER
BY HADDON CRAFTSMEN, BLOOMSBURG, PENNSYLVANIA

To Mira Son and Avalon Books for allowing me to
bring this story to print.

And especially to my parents, Bob and Lois Price, who have
always supported me, allowed me to explore my own path, and
showed me what a loving family is truly all about.
Thanks, Mom and Dad. I love you.

Chapter One

"Father, it's my vacation and I need to spend it in Texas," Marilyn Waters said into her cell phone.

"In Texas? To do what?"

"To fix up and sell Aunt Phoebe's house."

"Don't waste your time on that old dump! Call a real-estate agent. And vacation or not, I expect you back in Chicago, in the office, tomorrow morning at eight o'clock. Sharp!"

Marilyn winced. "Father, I can't. Please—"

A click and a dial tone were her response. He'd refused to listen—just like always.

Frustrated, she started to push the OFF button. Lightning split the late-afternoon sky, and she flinched, dropped the phone, and began to count. "One thousand one, one thousand two." Thunder exploded overhead, rattling the windows of her great-aunt's old farmhouse. She shuddered.

Oh, boy. Another storm.

Immediately, the North Texas skies burst open. Torrents of rain hammered the porch, and gale-force winds whipped tree limbs into a frenzy.

"It's just noise and light. I am *not* afraid of storms." Hugging herself, she drew a ragged breath. "Only the bad news that always follows."

That's why she couldn't sit still. Everything bad in her life had been foretold by a horrible thunderstorm, Aunt Phoebe's death included. What could have happened now? Her father was safe and sound in Chicago, and she had no other family.

She rubbed her arms, goose bumps evident through her suit jacket.

Twilight shadowed the foyer and she switched on a couple of lights. They glowed bright, casting an eerie glow on the dark wood floor, then flickered. Sighing, Marilyn turned back to the parlor. Forget getting a remodeling estimate today. No contractors in their right mind would come out in this weather.

The doorbell rang and she jumped. Who could that be? She crossed the hardwood floor to peer through the leaded glass and gasped at the familiar male figure shadowing the front porch.

Max? What's he doing here? Hannibal, Max's father, was supposed to come.

The doorbell pealed again. She straightened, plastered a neutral expression on her face, turned the handle, and opened the door. The wind caught it and flung it against the wall, forcing her to stumble backwards, and away from the last man she ever wanted to see.

Max Connors—the Connorsville, Texas, version of a Greek god—eyed her, his expression reserved.

Marilyn eyed him right back, unwilling to admit he could still unnerve her—and unable to tear her gaze from him.

Raven hair flowed straight back from his broad forehead. Angular cheekbones slashed his weather-tanned face. Dark brows framed even darker eyes. Energy and vigor radiated from his body, turning her knees to gelatin and her brain to mush.

Still. Even after fifteen years.

"Marilyn." A long pause. "It's been a long time."

Not long enough.

She opened her mouth to speak, to say hello, *anything,* but nothing came out. Max eyed her again, arching an ebony eyebrow.

Tongue-tied! Say something, Marilyn. Don't just stand there and ogle the man.

"Um, uh, hello, Max. Nice day, isn't it?"

Rain blew in the door, mocking her.

His other eyebrow shot up. "For fish, maybe."

"Of course, please come in." She motioned him inside, but he halted just over the threshold. The narrow foyer and hallway, dark from the heavy wood, surrounded them like a warm blanket. "I didn't expect you. I set up an appointment with Hannibal last week. Before I left Chicago. But then the rain. I mean, who'd want to get out in this weather?"

Great, she'd gone from tongue-tied to babbling.

Max looked her over. Once. Twice. She didn't blanch under his inky gaze, but she couldn't help feeling he still saw her as the ungainly teenager she'd been so long ago.

"Can't pour foundations in a deluge," he said, clearing his throat. "Good time to do interior work."

"Of course."

She closed the door and used it for support while she continued to study him. His thick hair trailed beyond his collar into a small ponytail held by a leather thong. The rain had flattened his silky mane to his head, emphasizing his angular face. Corded shoulder and back muscles strained against his water-darkened denim shirt.

Incredible. He appealed to her more now than the cocky college graduate who'd broken her heart that summer so long ago.

Clearly unaware of her scrutiny—thank goodness—he stepped past her to the walnut staircase and ran his broad palm over the hand-carved spindles and moldings. "My great-grandfather built this house," he said, his eyes glowing with pride. "The workmanship still amazes me."

"Yes," she said, echoing his awe, "it is beautiful."

"Pop said you wanted to fix this place up."

"That's correct." She paused, still unable to believe Aunt Phoebe had bequeathed her this lovely Victorian home. "Connors and Son built the house, so I thought Hannibal would be interested in getting it back on its feet. How's he been?"

A shadow darkened Max's face. "Pop's in the hospital."

"What!" Concern made her voice squeak. "Sondra said he was fine, and I spoke to him myself three days ago."

"My sister-in-law didn't want to worry you," he said. "Pop had a heart attack."

Marilyn's heart thumped and she sank onto a nearby gilt chair. There it was, the bad news that always followed the storm. Hannibal, the man who'd shown her the caring and concern her own father had withheld, was seriously ill.

"How . . . is he?" she asked, staring at her hands. "May I see him?"

"No."

She snapped her head up. "Why not?"

"He's still in intensive care. Until they move him to a private room, only family are allowed."

His words slapped her. She wasn't family; she didn't belong. Aunt Phoebe and the people in this small town were the only ones who'd ever showed her any affection, yet because she wasn't blood, she was an outsider. Like she'd been all her life.

Stop it, Marilyn! Self-pity never accomplished anything.

"I understand," she said, silently praying for Hannibal's quick recovery. "Will he be all right?"

Max glanced away. "He's stable, but it doesn't look good."

"Oh, Max. I am so sorry."

"Yeah."

She chewed her lip. If she'd known, she could have come sooner. She'd taken all her vacation leave to work on the house with Hannibal, to be with him one more time before she left Texas behind. Working with Max had never crossed her mind. Not Max.

Never Max.

"Well," he said, his voice husky, "shall we get down to it?"

Startled, she blinked. "Get down to what?"

"The house and what you want done to bring it up to code. To sell." He frowned. "Or are you going to live here?"

Live here? She could only dream! "I live and work in Chicago. I'm an executive recruiter on retainer for a large conglomerate called RSW, Inc."

"And?"

"And I'm going to sell."

He frowned deeper. "You're sure?"

"Yes," she said, confused by his expression. Surely he didn't want her to stay. *That* would be a dream come true. "Why? Is there a reason I shouldn't sell?"

"No, it just seems a shame to sell it," he said, running his hand over the carved staircase again. "Your family lived here a long time."

Her family? She'd never had one, at least not the kind he had: warm, loving. "I know, Max, but I don't have a choice."

"Right."

She *didn't* have a choice. Sure, selling meant breaking all ties with Texas, where this town, this house, and Aunt Phoebe had nurtured her and provided a safe haven from loneliness. But selling also meant she'd finally have enough money to start her own business, to get out from under her father, who, no matter how hard she tried, never let her get close. And though selling broke her heart, she had to take advantage of this opportunity to carve her own niche in life.

No one else would do it for her.

"As a builder you know the real estate market," she said after a few moments. "What are my chances?"

"Very good. People are moving here from the Dallas–Fort Worth Metroplex in droves, and every newcomer says the same thing. They love these Victorians. I bet you sell it before the work's finished."

"Well, that's good to hear," she said, not happy he now seemed more concerned about the house than her. Silly teenage crush! Marilyn took a calming breath and stood. "How long do you think the repairs will take?"

"Repairs?" He snapped his head around to focus his

inky gaze on her. "I thought you wanted to *restore* the entire house."

"Can't. Limited time. Limited budget."

"Right."

Max groaned inwardly. Budget restrictions were the bane of any contractor's existence, but that wasn't the only thing that had him worked up. Marilyn did, too. He couldn't believe how much she'd changed.

Stormy gray eyes gleamed at him from a creamy white face. Hair the color of honeyed oak hung loose, curving under at her shoulders, and touches of peach graced her cheeks and lips. Her skirted business suit outlined a trim, womanly body and showcased her long legs. Oh, yeah, little Marilyn Waters had definitely grown into an attractive woman.

Not interested.

Except he was, and to make matters worse, she still had that danged little-lost-puppy look—the one that made him want to protect her, to shield her from the big, bad world. To hold her in his arms.

Unbidden, his pulse picked up its beat.

"Have you checked out the renovations with the planning commission?" he asked, scolding himself for thinking of anything but business.

"No, I thought I'd get an idea of cost first. I may not have enough money to do the house justice."

Max *had* to restore this house. If Connors and Son wanted to keep up with the competition, he needed to expand. Historical renovation was the key to their survival, and Marilyn's house was the perfect jumping-off point.

"We'll begin with the basics," he said. "Structure, wiring, and plumbing. Then go from there."

"Fine."

The storm raged outside, a symphony of booms and crashes. Typical North Texas spring. He pulled a pad and pencil from his shirt pocket. "It's too wet to look at the exterior, but with this hard rain, we'll know if the roof leaks."

He started toward the stairs, but she didn't follow, didn't even move. Her gaze seemed stuck on the opposite wall.

"Marilyn? Are you coming?"

Her eyes widened. "You want me to inspect the house with you?"

"Yes, starting with the attic," he said, wishing she'd move so he could finish the estimate and get out. "I'm guessing a lot of the work will be cosmetic, but I've only been here a few times. You spent months with your aunt."

Still, she didn't move. Max looked her over. Rigid was an understatement. Could she hold a grudge against him after all these years? She certainly didn't seem happy to see him. Of course, that worked both ways.

Thunder boomed overhead, interrupting his thoughts. Marilyn flinched and his memory flew back fifteen years to his father's construction site. She'd been hanging around when a storm had blown in. From the first crash of thunder, she'd frozen in place and worn the same dazed look.

She was still afraid of storms?

Protective feelings kicked in, and he changed tactics. "We can start down here," he suggested, "and do the upstairs after the storm—"

"No," she said firmly. "We'll start at the top."

Determination tightened her expression and she strode toward the staircase. Max admired her guts, but when she reached his side a soft fragrance tickled his nose.

Roses. The light scent of summer roses washed over him and held him spellbound.

Warning bells rang in his head. They clanged and echoed until he no longer heard the mad rush of the wind.

Last time they'd met, Marilyn was a cute, wide-eyed, innocent teenager, tagging along and begging him to notice she was growing up. She'd been too young for him then. Now she was a career woman. Self-sufficient. Independent. Determined to make her mark in the world—alone.

Just like his ex-fiancée.

Well, he was determined, too—to save his family's business, and himself, from more heartache.

"Okay, I'll admit I'm curious," he said to ease the tension. "Town gossip says your aunt's attic is stuffed with antiques, and I'm anxious to steal a look at them."

"Of course." She nodded, then turned and strode up the walnut stairs, her black heels making muffled thumps on the carpeted treads. Lightning flashed and a tree limb scraped a nearby window. She flinched again, but didn't stop. "Come on, Max. Let's get this over with."

My thoughts exactly.

For two hours, Max examined the house. Admiration for Great-Grandpa Connors's carpentry skills grew with each room, as did his determination to do this house. No one but Connors and Son could do it justice, or deserved to. Excited, he made furious notes, almost forgetting that Marilyn trailed him everywhere he went. Almost.

They finished the tour on the first floor in the World War Two–era kitchen, the most structurally sound but least aesthetically pleasing room. "These cabinets are solid," Max said, "but I'd suggest stripping the green paint and refinishing them."

She ignored him. The storm had blown through and

she seemed calmer, but her gaze never quite met his. Good. He didn't want to be attracted to her—again.

"Marilyn?" he prompted, his ego getting in the way of his sense. "The cabinets?"

"Sorry. I was reminiscing." Her palm skimmed the scarred yellow countertop, and her eyes held a faraway look. "Aunt Phoebe and I baked dozens, maybe even hundreds of cookies here. Countless gallons of lemonade and iced tea."

The gentleness in her voice surprised him. He'd remembered her as quiet and sullen, as if being with her aunt was a chore. "I was sorry to hear about Phoebe. She was a great lady."

"Yes, she was. Thank you." Marilyn paused. "Some of those summers I spent here were the best of my life."

Again he was surprised—and curious. He leaned against the refrigerator, remembering one particular summer. "Only some?"

She stiffened. So, she remembered, too. Maybe storms weren't the only thing bothering her today.

The clouds lifted, allowing sunshine to flood the kitchen. Marilyn closed her eyes and stood in the beam of light, as if she drew strength from it, then turned to him, her gray eyes wide and...pleading? "Are we through?"

"For now." He straightened, and poked the pad and pencil into his pocket. "I'll inspect outside tomorrow."

"But—"

"Don't worry," he added, understanding and sharing her discomfort, "you don't have to be here."

"I wasn't worried, I..." She cleared her throat. "You'll call with the final estimate?"

"I'll leave a written copy in your mailbox."

"Thank you," she said, visibly relaxing. "Good-bye, Max."

"Good-bye."

Frustrated he'd reacted to her, and confused about her emotional display, he strode out of the kitchen and let himself out the front door. Once outside, he splashed through the puddles to his mud-splattered white Connors and Son pickup and headed for the hospital.

After she heard the door close, Marilyn slid down the cabinet into a tingling heap on the floor. She couldn't hire Max and work with him day after day. Not when she'd spend every moment recalling the summer she'd thrown herself at him and been summarily dismissed. Why couldn't Hannibal—

Wait. Hannibal was in the hospital. She had to know how he was. Concern restoring her strength, she pushed herself up off the black-and-white tile floor, retrieved her cell phone, and punched in her best friend's number.

Sondra answered on the second ring.

"Sondra Jensen Connors," Marilyn demanded, "I have a bone to pick with you."

"Lynnie? Where are you?"

"At Aunt Phoebe's house."

"What? Why? I thought you were going to call me with your flight info. I would have picked you up at the airport."

"I took an earlier flight." Marilyn sighed and settled onto a vinyl kitchen chair. "Would you have told me about Hannibal?"

"How did you find out?"

"Max told me."

"Max? When?"

"He was here giving me an estimate. *Instead* of Hannibal."

"Oh, Lynnie, I'm sorry." Sondra sighed. "You were so distraught last month at your aunt's funeral, I wanted you to stay in Chicago and rest. When we heard Phoebe left you the house, I knew you'd be back, so I waited. Forgive me?"

"Of course. You know I could never stay mad at you."

"So, when does Max start working on the house?"

"I haven't made that decision yet."

"What?" Sondra's voice rose a notch. "What's to decide?"

"Quick fix or entire restoration."

Sondra snorted. "Anybody can do a quick fix—"

Yes! Marilyn leapt to her feet. She didn't need Max's expertise, after all. Any builder could handle the repairs. "Thank you, Sondra, I hadn't thought of that."

"Marilyn Hope Waters. Don't tell me you're considering the competition. You might as well take food right out of my children's mouths."

Marilyn smiled. She loved Sondra like a sister, but the raven-haired beauty tended to exaggerate. Her husband, Max's younger brother Peter, was a successful lawyer who handled the Connorses' legal affairs, and had little to do with the construction company.

Connors and Son was Max's domain.

"Sondra, Max has no competition—"

"Ah, the plot thickens. Still tickles your fancy, does he?"

"I *meant,* no one in Connorsville works like he does. He's a master carpenter and very busy. Someone else might do the job quicker."

"Uh-huh."

"I'm thinking of my *budget.*"

"Yeah, right. Like that first summer we saw him."

Marilyn's breath caught and the image filled her mind like it was yesterday.

It was the summer she turned fourteen and she and Sondra went boy-watching at the newest housing subdivision. A myriad of machines whirred and buzzed. A dozen men yelled at one another over raucous music. Hammers punctuated the rock and roll. Hannibal greeted them like long-lost daughters, and cautioned them about safety.

She smiled and nodded at the older man, then glanced up—and saw Max.

Her heart thumped, and giddiness tickled her senses. He knelt on the roof, pounding shingles in the hot Texas sun. His movements were exact and effortless, graceful. She stood there mesmerized. When he turned and his pitch-black gaze bored into her, she nearly swooned and instantly fell in total teenage love.

"Lynnie?"

Sondra's voice jerked Marilyn back to the present. "That was a long time ago, Sondra."

"Hmmm, but memories linger."

"Sondra, I'm hanging up now."

"Okay, okay, I'll stop teasing. Want to come to supper?"

"I'd like to visit Hannibal."

"Good. He's been asking for you."

Affection flooded Marilyn. "When are visiting hours?"

"Anytime you want," Sondra said. "Connorsville Hospital wouldn't dare keep you out day or night. You're my best friend."

"But I'm not a relative." Max's words rang in her ears. Only family would be allowed to see Hannibal right now. How many times had she wished for a big loving family? A million or two.

Stop it, Marilyn. You wouldn't know what to do with a family, anyway. You have your career, be happy with that.

"I wouldn't feel right imposing on our friendship," she added. "I'll call the hospital—"

"No. I'll get a sitter for the kids and come pick you up right now. We'll visit Pop together."

Marilyn's spirits lifted. "Thank you. I appreciate it."

"Lynnie, I promise not to pressure you to hire Max, but—"

"I know," she said. "The Connorses are friends of Phoebe's family, and I should be loyal."

"Absolutely. Now, tell me, what did you think of Max?"

Marilyn blew out an exasperated breath. "Thought you weren't going to start that again."

"I'm serious. You've avoided him on all your visits—"

"I never avoided anyone."

"—so, you're able to judge better than those of us who see him every day. How did he look? Tired? Overworked?"

Magnificent.

"Overworked?" Marilyn echoed, Sondra's words penetrating her brain. "What do you mean, overworked?"

"I mean, Connors and Son are building six custom houses in that new subdivision. Hannibal frets, so Peter frets, so . . ."

"Ah, I get the picture," Marilyn said, warmed by the concern Sondra felt for her brother-in-law. "He looked fine to me."

"Good." Sondra's voice lightened, her relief evident. "See you in about half an hour."

Marilyn hung up the phone and stared out the kitchen window at her aunt's flower garden. Oh, the summers she'd spent out there: barbecuing, gardening, sunning. She'd visited often with her parents, but after her mother died, her father had sent her alone—every summer—to get her out of his hair. Marilyn had hated being dismissed, but loved Texas, this house, and her aunt. Phoebe was a stoic, quiet woman but knew everyone in town and made sure Marilyn met them all—especially Sondra. Those visits during her teenage years had been idyllic, a fantasy, and she'd dubbed them her Lone Star Adventure.

Of course, after spying Max on that rooftop and falling inexplicably in puppy love, her Lone Star Adventure had taken on mythic proportions.

Selling Aunt Phoebe's house would end the adventure, but what else could Marilyn do? To have a future, she had to sell. To sell, she had to fix the house. To fix the house—she had to hire Max. No matter what her concerns, she had no choice. Sondra and Hannibal came closer to family than anything Marilyn had ever had, and she loved them deeply. Disappointing them wasn't an option.

So, her decision was clear. Hire Max, and guard herself from his appeal. Nothing to it. Piece of cake. No problem.

Oh, boy, if only it were that simple.

Max lounged in a chrome-and-vinyl chair next to his father's hospital bed. In the quiet, a heart monitor beeped, oxygen hissed faintly, and a nurse spoke in low tones with an orderly. Hannibal Connors lay on white sheets, round pads stuck to his chest, with a green-tinted tube in his nose.

He looked frail and old—totally opposite of the vigorous man he'd always been.

"Did you see Marilyn?" he asked, his voice raspy and faint.

"I looked over the house's interior," Max said. "I'm going back tomorrow to do the rest."

"That's not what I meant. How'd she look?"

Great.

He shrugged. "Like Marilyn."

Pop struggled to sit, so Max adjusted the bed. "I meant, how's she holding up? Phoebe's death had to be a blow."

"Tired," he answered, as his mind flashed back to Marilyn's luminous gray eyes, and the slight circles underneath. Funny how he hadn't noticed them then. "The storm upset her, too."

"Poor darlin'. When do you start renovating?"

"Maybe never."

"What?"

Hannibal jerked upright, dislodging a monitor lead. Max leaped to his feet. An alarm whined, and a nurse hurried in to make the necessary adjustments.

Dr. Allan Randalls, a tall, redheaded man about Max's age, strolled in as the nurse exited. "You must be feeling better," he teased. "That's the third time you've disconnected yourself."

"I'd like to yank them all off," Hannibal grumbled.

Dr. Randalls nodded. "I understand, but it won't be much longer now. Be patient." He made a note on the chart, glanced at Max, then nodded toward the door. Max followed until they were out of earshot of the coronary care unit.

Allan turned to him. "Max, I've recommended to your father that he retire."

"What? Why?"

"His heart took quite a beating with this attack. Add the complications of hypertension—"

"You mean high blood pressure? Since when?"

"Since I diagnosed him years ago." Allan frowned. "I'm not surprised you didn't know. Hannibal doesn't take his medication, or watch what he eats. After your mother passed away, I got the impression your father simply stopped taking care of himself."

Familiar grief tightened Max's chest. Angela Connors's death had stripped Hannibal's lighthearted spirit. The whole family had suffered, but Pop had withdrawn from life, using work as solace. Only when his children or grandchildren surrounded him did he show any sparks of enthusiasm.

"Six years," Max muttered. "Pop's had problems for six years and never said a word."

"If I thought he'd slow down, work part-time—"

"Not a chance. Not in a million years."

"I know." Allan blew out a breath. "Talk to him, Max. Maybe you can get him to understand. Until we get him back on his feet, he needs to avoid stress—of any kind."

Max nodded, watched Allan walk away, then stared at the diamond patterns on the tile floor, guilt weighting his shoulders. Had he been working so hard he hadn't noticed Pop's health problems? Could this attack have been avoided? And what would his father do without work? Then a dash of anger set in. Why hadn't Pop said anything?

Max rubbed a hand over his jaw, and strode back into his father's room.

The older man raised up. "Well, when do I check out of this poor excuse for a pincushion factory?"

"Soon. But you need to take your medication this time."

"So, young Allan spilled the beans." Hannibal groaned. "That doctor is worse than an old woman."

"*That doctor* says take your medicine and avoid stress."

"Just sign me out and let me get back to work."

"Sorry, Pop," Max said gently. "Time to hang up your tool belt."

His father paled and shrank into the mattress. "I'd rather die."

"Don't talk like that."

"I'll go nuts without something to do. Besides, you've got six houses to build in that new subdivision, plus redo Marilyn's. I'm not dumping all that work on you."

Max laid a hand on his father's shoulder, and was relieved to feel strong muscles bunch underneath. "I can handle it. You've been training me to take over the business since you first put a hammer in my hand."

"You were three," Hannibal said, managing a slight grin. "Thought that hammer was best toy you ever got. You even slept with it."

"Still do," Max quipped.

Hannibal laughed, and dislodged another lead. The nurse rushed in, frowned, then relaxed when she saw the men laughing.

"Believe me, Max," Hannibal said, his face clouding, "I'll go nuts without something to do."

"How about taking care of yourself? According to Allan, staying healthy will be a full-time job."

"Bull."

"Then hang out with your grandchildren. You bellyache about it enough. Take time to see Pete's kids."

His father raised an eyebrow. "What about you? When are you going to find some nice girl and get some kids of your own?"

"Never." Max set his jaw, tired of the same old argument. "Pete's your married son and has three children. Let it go at that."

"A wife could do the books and that paperwork you hate so much."

"I'm not going to get married to get a bookkeeper."

"So the business will die with you, is that it? The name of the company, in case you hadn't noticed, is Connors *and Son.* Why do you have trouble remembering that?"

How could he forget?

His home, the hundred-year-old Connors homestead, had been lovingly built for a bride and for the sons and daughters that followed. Each board, each nail, every inch of plaster reminded Max he'd avoided marriage and children.

"Why do *you* have trouble remembering that Pete has two sons to carry on the family tradition?" Max asked. "Not to mention you have another son in college. Alex is only twenty, with his whole future ahead of him."

Hannibal snorted. "Connors tradition demands the business goes from eldest son to eldest son."

Max sighed. He and his father shared the same powerful build, the same dark looks, and the same loyalty toward family. Except for this one point.

"Pop, we've been through this before. I don't want to get married. I got close, once. It was a disaster."

"Not all women are like Brittany. Dang it, Max, you're great with Pete's kids, why pass up a chance to be a father?"

"Because being an uncle suits me just fine." Once upon a time, Max *had* wanted a wife and children, but Brittany convinced him he was fooling himself.

"Liar. You're just letting one bad experience eat at you like termites gnawing wood. Smoke 'em out! Get back to building yourself a life."

"There's nothing to smoke out," Max insisted, "and I'm too busy to build anything other than houses."

"Humph." Hannibal grimaced, then arched a gray eyebrow. "What about Marilyn?"

Max blinked, trying to ignore the image of Marilyn's honey-gold hair and soft gray eyes. He didn't want to think about her. She was like Brittany, his ex-fiancée, too wrapped up in her career to notice anything else. He couldn't believe she wanted to sell her aunt's house. Didn't she realize that Victorian was a historic treasure, a symbol of her family?

"What about her?" Max retorted finally.

"You've got to restore that house. It's a masterpiece of my grandfather's craftsmanship. The staircase, the molding—"

"I know, Pop," Max said, glad they were back to discussing business instead of marriage. "When I inspected it today, I stepped back in time. Nobody does that kind of work anymore."

"You can. I'm telling you, Max, you're my grandpa reborn. You've got his touch."

Yeah, Max had carpentry in his blood—four generations' worth—and he liked it, loved working with his hands. He kept Great-Grandpa Connors's tools sharp and in good shape, and occasionally used them to replace a spindle or repair a broken molding. Restoring an entire house was his personal dream.

"Marilyn is on a limited budget," he added after a few moments. "She wants to fix it up enough to sell."

"I don't care what her budget is," Hannibal insisted, "you make sure she gives you that contract. With the whole town restoration-crazy, her house will set up Connors and Son—you—for a truckload of business. Then me and my blood pressure could forget about those greedy Dallas builders moving up here and underbidding us."

"I'll talk to her tomorrow."

"You'll *convince* her tomorrow."

Hannibal's face reddened and Max relented. "Okay, Pop, okay. I'll convince her tomorrow. Leave it to me."

"Good." Hannibal relaxed against the pillows. "Now get out of here and let me get some rest."

Max bid his father good night, strolled into the hallway, and sagged against the wall. He couldn't complete his estimate on Marilyn's house until he checked the outside, but so far the structure looked sound. He wouldn't be the only builder itching to get his hands on it, though.

How did he guarantee to underbid the competition? If he offered to do some of the work at cost, he might convince her to renovate the entire place. Yeah. He could afford a small profit now to gain a larger one later.

Confident, he straightened, only to have a thought strike him. Sure, he could afford a cut now, but could he afford to be near Marilyn day in and day out for months? She touched something in him. What, he didn't know. Maybe, like with Brittany, he hoped a soft-hearted woman existed under Marilyn's self-serving exterior. Or maybe he still felt protective of the shy, gangly teenager that had tagged after him.

Whatever the reason, being around Marilyn would be

tough. To keep the family business booming, though, he'd grit his teeth and do it. Because for him, family meant everything.

Resigned, he headed for the elevators. Tonight he'd work on the estimate.

Tomorrow, he'd work on Marilyn.

Chapter Two

At that moment, Marilyn clutched the chrome railing of the hospital elevator. White lab coats, the squeak of rubber-soled shoes, and the unmistakable odor of disinfectant overwhelmed her senses, reminding her of the night her mother died. She squeezed her eyes shut to block out the memories of death, then took a deep breath. Hannibal wasn't going to die. She had to believe that.

"Lynnie, you okay?"

Marilyn sighed, then gazed into Sondra's concerned blue eyes. "I'm not crazy about hospitals, but I'm fine."

Sondra put an arm around her shoulders. "Maybe we should come back another time. You've had a long day, flying and everything."

"I can't. Knowing's better than not knowing."

"I understand, and I'm right here if you need me."

"Thank you."

They reached the fourth floor and the elevator opened. A dark, familiar figure stood on the other side.

Marilyn gulped. Max looked more handsome than he had earlier. Was that possible?

"Hiya, Max," Sondra said brightly. "How's Pop?"

"Hey, Sondra. Marilyn." Max stepped back to let them off the elevator, his eyes narrowed with concern. "He's better. Tired, but better."

"Thank goodness." Sondra sighed. "Think he's too tired to talk to Lynnie?"

Max looked her over, the concerned gaze deepening. Marilyn stiffened. "I guess it's all right," he said finally. "He's been asking about her."

She blew out a breath. "Thank you, Max. I couldn't sit at home—at Aunt Phoebe's—just wondering."

"Yeah," he said, his deep voice rumbling in his chest. "Knowing's better than not knowing."

"That's just what Lynnie said." Sondra winked. "Great minds think alike, huh?"

Max arched an eyebrow. "Right."

Marilyn blinked, but said nothing. She couldn't. Her throat had closed up. She and Max had something in common? Since when?

Sondra laid a hand on Max's arm. "Come for supper, Max. Then you can come back and visit Pop again later tonight."

"Thanks, but I gotta check on my crew. Make sure they battened down the Ferguson house after that storm." He paused. "Then I've got a mile-high stack of paperwork."

"Come on, Max," Sondra coaxed, "you know my food's better than that drive-through junk you scarf down."

He darted a glance at Marilyn. "Well, I don't know."

"Do what you need to do, then drop by the house," Sondra insisted. "Lynnie and I are going to visit with Pop, then we'll scoot on home. Probably have supper on the table about the time your belly starts growling."

He arched an eyebrow. "You going to be there, Marilyn?"

"I guess."

"Sure she is," Sondra insisted. "I'm not going to let her eat by herself her first night back in town."

"I'll be there." He turned to Marilyn. "I need to talk to you."

She chewed her lip. "You do?"

"About your aunt's house."

"Of course."

Disappointment clogged her throat, and she scolded herself. She really had to get over Max. She'd matured, grown way beyond teenage crushes. Besides, he hadn't wanted her fifteen years ago. He wouldn't want her now.

After what had transpired in the past fifteen years, no man would want her. Ever.

"Check ya later, Max," Sondra said.

Max nodded and walked away.

Sondra tugged on Marilyn's hand. "Let's see how Pop's doing."

Marilyn followed, but her focus strayed to the view over her shoulder. Max stood waiting for the elevator, arms crossed over his chest. He looked so strong, so solid. Her heart skittered a beat or two. She was glad he'd be at dinner with Sondra and Peter. They could discuss the house without being alone.

She stumbled, and caught herself on the counter of the nurse's station.

"Eyes forward, young lady," Sondra quipped. "Not on someone behind you."

Marilyn blushed. "I was surprised to run into him, that's all."

"Figuratively—and almost literally. Let's see, how many times does that make? Twice in the same day after not seeing him for what, six years? Yes, since Peter's and my wedding, where as one of the wedding party, you couldn't possibly avoid him." Sondra winked. "Yep, twice in one day. Must be fate."

"Merely a coincidence. And I haven't avoided anyone."

Sondra rolled her eyes. "Uh-huh."

Marilyn *had* avoided Max, though. Every time she came to visit Aunt Phoebe or Sondra after that awful summer, Marilyn had made sure she was where Max wasn't. After a few years, she got busy with college and her career and the visits became less frequent. Avoiding Max then, who was even busier than Marilyn, was quite easy.

Thank goodness.

Marilyn straightened. "Can we see Hannibal now?"

"Coincidence?" Sondra tapped her finger to her lips. "Hmm, twice in the same day. What are the odds?"

"Sondra, please stop."

"Lynnie?" Her eyes widened. "I'm sorry. You know I don't mean anything by it."

"I know," Marilyn said, slightly ashamed of herself. Sondra teased the people she liked. Normally, it made Marilyn feel better, but not today. "I guess I'm more on edge than I thought," she added. "I'm sorry. Can we see Hannibal?"

"Are you family?" the nurse asked.

"You bet she is," Sondra insisted. "Come on, Lynnie."

Sondra's words warmed Marilyn. If only it were that

easy. But being part of a family meant more than sneaking in to see a sick friend—a lot more.

Sighing, she followed Sondra down the hall. Three walls and a curtain formed Hannibal's room. A strange machine whooshed in the corner and a heart monitor beeped on a shelf next to the bed. Sondra approached him, but Marilyn halted on the threshold. He looked so pale, so tired. Max had said Hannibal was better.

Marilyn's hand flew to her throat. Better than what?

He looked up. "Marilyn Waters, you're as pretty as new-poured concrete."

Sondra giggled. "Oh, Pop, what a thing to say."

"You ever see concrete when it's newly dried? Looks just like silver—all shiny and clean."

Marilyn quickly moved to his side. "Thank you. It's good to see you."

"It's good to be seen," he retorted.

She kissed his cheek, then smoothed her skirt. She'd intended to change out of her business clothes, but she'd been too anxious to see Hannibal.

He glanced from her to Sondra. "Both my daughters at once. Now that's the best medicine a man could have."

Tears sprang to Marilyn's eyes. Since she'd served as Sondra's maid of honor, Hannibal had called her his other daughter—Sondra being the first. If only it were true.

"I would have been here sooner," she said, "but I didn't know you were ill until this afternoon."

"My fault," Sondra explained. "She's been through so much, I didn't want to worry her."

"Darn tootin'." Hannibal squeezed Marilyn's hand. "Sit down. Visit with me a while before that battle-ax of a nurse shoos you away."

"I know you two want to talk," Sondra said, "so I'll wait for Lynnie in the hall."

Marilyn mouthed a thank you, sat in a nearby chair, and continued to hold Hannibal's hand. His fingers felt cold and stiff. "Are you really all right?" she asked.

"I will be after you tell me what Max did to rile you up."

She blinked. "I'm not angry with Max."

"Don't kid me, you two have avoided each other for years."

"I'm not angry with Max," she repeated, tired of the avoidance issue. She *wasn't* angry with Max. Disappointed, frustrated, wary, maybe, but not angry.

"Then why didn't you put your John Hancock on a contract?"

Marilyn searched the older man's face. How could she justify her need to get back to Chicago without sounding selfish? "I don't have a lot of time or money, Hannibal."

"Call me Pop," he said. "Job giving you a hard time?"

She nodded. "I want to open my own agency. The quicker I sell Aunt Phoebe's house, the sooner I can get out—"

"On your own." Hannibal squeezed her hand. "Working for your father didn't get you close to him, did it?"

"I . . . It . . ." She paused and shook her head. "You really cut right to it, don't you?"

"I'm old," he said with a grin. "Don't have time to beat around the bush."

"He's . . . his company is so sterile, impersonal. They need bodies to fill their slots, so they call me. They don't care about the person, just the résumé." She glanced away. "If I strike out on my own, I can—"

"Add the personal touch?"

"Yes."

"So start here."

She dropped his hand and stared him. "In Connorsville?"

Both gray eyebrows shot up. "You got something against my town? Or Texas?"

"Of course not, but..."

"Then fix up that old place and move here where you belong."

Where you belong. The words swirled around her mind like a dream, but she had to wake up. With Aunt Phoebe gone, she had no family connection to Connorsville, and she didn't want to depend on friends.

Besides, she had to do this on her own, to prove to her father—and to herself—that she could be successful.

"I have to sell," she said. "If I don't, I won't have the start-up capital. As to Texas, well, all my contacts are in Chicago."

He took her hand again. "Then let Max give that old farmhouse his personal touch. You know he can."

"Yes," she said slowly, "I saw the rocking chair he made for Sondra when Baby Peter was born. Max is very talented."

"So, what's stopping you?"

"Hannibal—"

"Pop."

"—it's not that easy." Marilyn swallowed. "Pop."

"I tell you what's easy and what's not. Easy is signing that contract. Not easy is watching you sell that house and cut all ties with this town." He narrowed his eyes. "So what's it going to be? You going to be sensible and stay, or cause me some of that stress that old woman of a doctor says I can't have?"

Marilyn's jaw dropped, then she caught the mischief

in Hannibal's gaze and rolled her eyes. "That's a low blow," she said. "You're playing on my sympathies."

His black eyes sparkled. "I'm playing on what gets me my way."

How could she refuse him anything? She loved him. If he wanted her to fly to the moon, she'd flap her arms until they dropped off. But in this situation, she had to be realistic. Starting in Chicago would take less money and less time. And she could be independent there.

Connorsville wouldn't allow her to remain aloof. The town would draw her in, and she'd get hurt—again.

"My budget has its limits," she hedged.

"Talk to Max. He'll give you a good deal."

"Pop, you're not being fair," Marilyn began, then an idea struck her. "All right, I'll talk to him on one condition. *You* follow the doctor's orders."

"Ah, darlin', that's *really* not fair."

She arched an eyebrow, and imitated his deep voice. "You wouldn't want to cause me some stress, would you?"

"Well, I'll be switched. You got me over a barrel there." He sighed. "Okay, darlin', you got a deal."

"Good." She rose to leave. "Get better quickly, please?"

"One more thing." To her surprise, his face clouded over. "I never told you this, but you remind me of my wife. Do you remember her?"

Marilyn nodded, too choked up to speak. Angela Connors had been a sweet, quiet woman, the type that kept the boisterous Connors men in line with a look or a word.

"She was gentle like you," he said, his voice full of emotion. "She had quiet, expressive eyes like you, too. I loved her so much."

"I know you did," she whispered. "Everyone knew it. She had a soft nature and a smile to match. I admired her."

"This heart attack got me thinking about her. I've had a good life, darlin'. I want my children to have the same."

"They will, and do." She frowned, concerned he was more seriously ill than he let on. "Peter has Sondra and the children. Alex will graduate soon and start his architect's career."

Hannibal grimaced. "And Max will die alone."

"What?" She chewed her lip, realizing Hannibal was truly worried. "But everyone likes Max, Pop."

"Humph."

She softened her voice, eager to ease his concern. "Maybe he hasn't found the right woman yet."

Hannibal turned away, his voice gruff. "He ain't looking. And it's all that Brittany's fault."

Marilyn flinched, then forced a smile on her face and left the room.

As soon as she stepped into the hall, fierce jealousy gripped her.

Who in the world was Brittany?

Max sat in his pickup and stared for a full five minutes at his brother Pete's sprawling brick home. Should he go in, or call and back out of supper? He'd had a long, hard day. Thanks to the spring rains—and the Fergusons constantly changing their minds—his six custom homes in the Wildwood subdivision had fallen weeks behind schedule. He needed to talk to Marilyn, but he didn't have the energy to fight his attraction to her.

He started to leave, then realized talking to her in Peter

and Sondra's company would buffer the tension. He hoped.

The minute he walked into the house, however, he regretted his decision.

"Hiya, Max," Sondra said. "Thank goodness you're here. Everything's gone to pot since Lynnie and I got home from the hospital."

He glanced around the cozy and normally immaculate kitchen. His two-year-old niece, Emily, sat in her pink-and-purple high chair banging a symphony on the plastic tray with a spoon, her mouth a rainbow mosaic of splattered food. Four-year-old Joseph sat in his fire engine booster seat, coloring on a napkin—linen from the looks of it—and Baby Peter wailed from a *Sesame Street* playpen in the corner.

"The crew mutiny on you?" he asked.

"Very funny." Sondra swiped a strand of black hair from her forehead. "This is normal. Joseph, stop coloring on that. Use the paper Mommy gave you." She sighed. "Peter's car broke down and he's had it towed. I have to pick him up at the service station, except my restaurant called and two hostesses quit. They're short-handed, and the high school baseball team is celebrating their end of the season tonight. I have to be at three places at once and I'm certain I burned supper."

The odor of scorched pasta wafted across his nose. "Well, I can't do anything about the food, but I can go get Pete."

Marilyn walked in. She'd removed her suit jacket, revealing a white silk blouse with a wet spot on one shoulder. Max stared. She looked softer, more approachable than she had that afternoon.

She didn't see him yet, and continued to dab at the wet spot with a small towel. "I don't think it's going to stain, Sondra," she said. Then she looked up. "Oh, hi, Max."

"Baby Peter spit up on Lynnie," Sondra explained to him. "You know how he is with strangers."

Marilyn crossed her arms as if she needed to cover herself. "Guess I'm not good with children."

"Nonsense," Sondra said. "Emily and Joseph think you're great. Baby Peter suffers from stranger anxiety."

Max turned to leave. He didn't want to stay and notice how soft Marilyn looked or hear how good she was with his niece and nephews. He needed to label her as a determined career woman, to stem his attraction.

He dug his truck keys out of his jeans pocket. "I'll go get Pete."

"No." Sondra laid a hand on his arm. "I'd rather you baby-sat. Once I get Peter, he can take me to the restaurant, then come on home."

Max arched an eyebrow. "You expect *me* to fix supper for these guys?" He hated to cook. Loved to eat, but unless it involved a barbecue and lighter fluid, he steered clear of meal preparation.

"I'll do it," Marilyn said quickly. "Max knows the children, and can keep them entertained."

Sondra took off her apron and handed it over to Marilyn like handing over the throne of a kingdom. "Thanks, Lynnie, you're a peach." She kissed each of the kids. "You be good while I'm gone," she told them and headed out the back door. Before it closed behind her she stopped and winked. "That includes the adults, too."

Max shrugged, then headed for Baby Peter. Marilyn came toward him, grazing his body as they passed each other. His right side buzzed and he caught her rose-fresh scent again. He frowned. "What do you think?" he said, reaching into the playpen.

"About what?"

"Supper."

She gazed into the pot and grimaced. "I hate to say it about a great restauranteur like Sondra, but this spaghetti is a lost cause." To his surprise, she dumped it down the sink, then began to rummage through the pantry and the refrigerator. "Better start fresh."

She hummed while she worked, thoroughly ignoring him. This morning he could have sworn she'd felt the connection between them. Had he imagined it? He watched her as she glided effortlessly around the kitchen, then shook his head. She didn't even know he was there.

"You like to cook?" he asked over the baby's screams.

"Oh, yes," she said, "though it's not much fun for one person."

Did that mean she didn't have a man in her life? He hadn't seen a ring on her finger, and Sondra would have mentioned a boyfriend. . . . Max shook his head again. What did he care? Marilyn's personal life was none of his business.

Baby Peter quieted a bit, and Max settled him back into the playpen where the boy studied his toes. Emily dropped her spoon. The resulting quiet fell on the room like a ton of bricks. "Exactly why I manage to impose on Pete at suppertime," he said.

She stopped chopping a head of lettuce and arched a tawny eyebrow. "Is it?"

"Is it what?"

"An imposition for you to be here. You're family."

He laughed. "According to Sondra it is. She calls me the 'Sorry Old Bachelor.' "

Marilyn's gray eyes widened. "You're kidding."

"Ever since Pop moved out of the homestead, all I hear is 'Poor old Max. All alone.' " He grinned. " 'Has to depend on his younger brother for a nourishing meal.' "

She relaxed and smiled. Max's pulse doubled. She had a soft, sweet smile that lit up her face.

"Oh, she teases you." Marilyn put the lettuce aside, then measured some frozen peas into a saucepan. "That I understand."

"Yeah?" He arched an eyebrow. "What does Sondra tease you about?"

"Are we having peas?" Joseph asked.

"Yes, we are, sweetie." Marilyn's voice flowed like honey. "Do you like peas?"

"They look like wittle green balls," he said. Then he grinned. "I'm drawing you a picher, Uncle Max."

"On the paper, I hope." He lifted one of the four-year-old's arms and tried to peer under it.

Joseph didn't let him. "It's not done. You can't look."

"Okay, Squirt, whatever you say." He kissed the boy's dark head, then turned to his left to pick up Emily's dropped spoon.

"Don't give it back to her," Marilyn said quickly. "The noise is deafening."

Instead, Max handed her *his* spoon. The toddler gleefully began banging again.

Marilyn arched an eyebrow. "Doesn't that bother you?"

"Nah. After listening to nail guns, power saws, and backhoes, this is nothing."

"Oh, I hadn't thought of that."

"Not used to being around children?" He gently replaced Emily's spoon with a paper napkin. His niece paused for a moment, then just as happily began to shred it into tiny pieces.

Marilyn froze, her face so stricken Max wondered if she'd seen a ghost. "Marilyn? You okay?"

"No. I mean, I'm fine, and um, children aren't a part of my regular routine."

The phone rang and she nearly fell over her own feet to answer it. Apparently, he'd upset her with his question. Why? Brittany had at least been upfront about it.

Max watched her face as she spoke into the phone, trying to figure her out.

"Connors residence," she said quietly. "No, he's not at home. His brother, Max, is here." Her hand reached toward him to give him the receiver, but stopped. "No? Then, may I take a message? Certainly. Thank you for your concern."

She hung up and flushed all over, as if she were embarrassed.

He arched an eyebrow. "Who was that?"

"Brittany Sawyer."

Anger and old hurt flared in his gut. "What did *she* want?"

"She heard about your father."

Max narrowed his eyes. Why did his ex-fiancée call now? She'd never cared one whit about his father when she lived in Connorsville. "How? What did she say?"

Marilyn sank onto the wooden chair near the phone. "She saw Alex yesterday in Austin. He was sketching the front of the hotel she was staying in."

"Thought she was in New York," he said absently, still intent on Marilyn. Why did she blush? "Anything else?"

"She passed on her get-well wishes and hung up."

"Good."

"Why didn't she want to talk to you?"

"Here's your picher, Uncle Max," Joseph said suddenly.

Max took the masterpiece, glad for the interruption. He didn't want to talk or even think about Brittany. She'd never understood about the Connors family ties, never accepted that he couldn't leave Connorsville and the family business.

They'd split up when she received a job offer in New York and had expected him to pack up and move.

"Now, what do we have here?" he asked.

"It's you, Uncle Max." Joseph climbed into his lap to point out the specific features of his drawing. "See, this is Mommy and Daddy and me and Em'ly and the baby."

Max searched the multicolored squiggles. "Where am I?"

"In the corner, by yourself."

Great, now even his nephew was taunting him. Was it bred in the genes, this haranguing about marriage and children?

"Do you like it, Uncle Max?" Joseph peered up at him, blue eyes wide with eagerness.

"I sure do, Squirt." He hugged him. "You look so much like your mommy."

"Mommy's a girl," Joseph insisted. "I don't look like a girl."

Emily giggled. "Jo-Jo wook wike a girl."

Marilyn leaned forward and said softly, "Uncle Max means you have black hair and pretty blue eyes like your mommy."

Joseph thought about that for a moment, then gave Max a hug and a kiss. "Thank you, Uncle Max."

Max moved him back to his booster seat. "Thank *you* for my picture." Carefully folding the paper, he placed it in his shirt pocket and patted the material. "I'll keep it next to my heart."

Marilyn returned to the stove, and in a few minutes set peas, applesauce, and stir-fry chicken in front of Max and Joseph. Emily wore most of hers, so Marilyn warmed some more and tried to feed her. "Max?"

"Hmm?" Every bite was delicious, and melted in his mouth. "Maybe you should go into the restaurant business yourself."

"Thank you, but I don't have Sondra's touch." She scooped the last bit of food into Emily's mouth and added, "Who's Brittany?"

He paused, his fork in mid-air.

"I ask because your father mentioned her this afternoon."

"To you?"

She winced and looked stricken again. For the life of him, he didn't understand why.

"He's worried about you, about all of his family," she said. "His heart attack started him thinking."

"About what?"

She took a wet cloth, cleaned Emily's face, then whispered, "He's afraid . . . um, maybe we shouldn't talk about this in front of the children."

Max looked at his niece and nephews. All three, even Baby Peter, focused their wide eyes on the adults. "Maybe you're right. Let's get these guys cleaned up and ready for bed."

"Um, uh, I'll take care of the dishes."

He frowned. "I know children aren't part of your regular routine, but I could use the help. Emily and Joseph are both going to need a bath. Baby Peter, too."

"Well . . ."

He watched her, waiting for her to back out. Brittany

had never liked children. Insisted they were "too messy" for a cultured woman. Marilyn looked softer without her suit jacket, but would she be willing to get messy?

"But it won't take a minute to clean this up," she insisted.

"Fine," he said, disappointed. "I'll handle it."

"I won't be a minute, really."

Max left the room to gather the bath things, agitated. Why had he expected Marilyn to jump at the chance to bathe the kids? To prove she wasn't like Brittany? He shook his head. He didn't care. Marilyn had her life and he had his. Better to leave it that way, and expect nothing.

Marilyn watched him go, knowing he was upset with her and unsure why. To make amends, she quickly loaded the dishwasher, wiped the table, and swept up the peas that had missed Joseph's mouth and fallen onto the floor. She wished she had changed into jeans. Her skirt and blouse were inappropriate for bathing children. How could she move around?

She chewed her lip, anxious. She hadn't told Max the entire truth about her experience with children. She had none. Zip. Zero. Zilch. Except for her rare visits to Sondra's, Marilyn had never even held a baby. Tonight, she'd tried desperately to feed Baby Peter and botched that.

She wanted to be good with them, though, and knew she had to try again. Deciding her pumps would only hinder her, she kicked off her shoes and hurried down the hall to the Southwestern-style bathroom. Giggles and squeals filled the air, along with the smell of scented bubbles. The turquoise ceramic tub resembled a swimming pool with Max as its very wet lifeguard. Water glistened in his hair and darkened the front of his shirt and jeans. He glanced up as she entered, and her heart stopped.

He was the picture of fatherhood. Caring. Loving. Devoted. Had Brittany hurt him so much, he'd decided never to marry and have children of his own? Marilyn swallowed. She was beginning to hate Brittany. No one should affect Max that way. He'd make a great dad.

He eyed her a moment, surprise evident in his gaze. Finally, he grinned. "Hard to tell who's bathing whom, isn't it?"

She grinned back, unable to help herself. "How can I help?"

He eyed her again, his gaze resting on her shoeless, hose-covered feet. "Grab a kid and start scrubbing."

"All right."

She moved into the room. Joseph and Emily splashed happily while Baby Peter cooed in his small carrier near the door. Apparently they were unaware a novice baby-bather was in their midst. Still, Marilyn knelt on the patterned rug next to Max. Only a few inches separated them, but she didn't allow herself to draw back. Instead, she rolled up her sleeves, plunged right in, and shampooed Emily's blond curls.

"Their skin is so soft," she whispered. "I had no idea."

"Yeah, they smell good, too," Max said. "When they're clean, anyway," he added. He poured a cup of water over Joseph's dark hair, taking care to shield the boy's eyes.

They worked side by side, first Joseph and Emily together, then Baby Peter in a separate plastic tub. Marilyn's heart pounded; she was afraid she'd make one of the children cry, but she didn't give up. She watched Max, and tried hard to mimic his movements.

Finally, all three children had been bathed, shampooed, and dried. Marilyn couldn't believe it. Nobody had screamed or thrown a tantrum, so she must have done all right. While Max dressed them and put them to bed, she stood and took stock of the results of her first baby-bathing experience. Soapsuds covered her from fingertip to elbow and a water stain ran the length of her skirt.

"What a mess," she said when Max returned.

"I'm sorry you got wet," Max said gruffly.

"Sorry? Why?" Marilyn swiped a tendril of hair from her cheek. "I loved it."

Max stared at her, both raven eyebrows arched. "You did?"

"Oh, yes." She picked up a towel and glanced around the room. "But I've seen pictures of floods that left less damage. "Is this . . . aftermath normal?"

His expression lightened, as if he'd just heard great news, then he rolled his eyes. "This is nothing. Thanks to you, we averted hurricane-force destruction."

Her jaw nearly dropped. "Thanks to me?"

"Yeah," he said, taking the towel from her. "Easiest bath time ever."

"Thank you." She grinned, genuinely pleased. "Next time, though, I'll wear a scuba suit."

He stared at her a moment, then laughed, his rich voice echoing off the tiles. "Hmmm, maybe a mask, too. Here, let me."

Before she understood his motives, he took the corner of the towel and reached toward her. Time slowed and her senses heightened. His hand caressed her skin through the terry cloth as it slid millimeter by millimeter down her nose. The fragrance of cherry-scented soap mixed with Max's outdoor scent.

She closed her eyes, knowing she'd stepped into heaven.

How could Brittany have let him get away?

"There," he said, "all clean."

"Thank you." Her eyes popped open and she gazed into amused black eyes. "Dirt or food?"

"Bubble bath."

"A normal hazard of the job?"

"You keep asking that." He knit his eyebrows. "Haven't you ever bathed kids before?"

"No."

"Could have fooled me." He peered at her. "Marilyn, you're a natural. You really ought to have some of your own."

Her throat closed up, but she held back the tears. His simple praise shot pain right to her soul. "I'll keep that in mind," she said hoarsely.

"Marilyn, what—" Baby Peter cried and Max headed down the hall. "I thought he went to sleep a little too easily."

Marilyn followed, watching with awe as Max leaned over the crib and gently pulled Baby Peter into his arms. "You cutting teeth, buddy?" Max murmured. "Want Uncle Max to rock you?"

"May I?" she whispered, her voice ragged. "He and I didn't get off to a very good start. I'd really like to try again."

He gave her that "just heard great news" expression again and nodded. "Sure. Sit in the rocker and I'll hand him to you."

She settled herself in the polished walnut rocking chair and Max gently laid Baby Peter in her arms. She stiffened at first, afraid he'd fuss. Instead, he snuggled against her shoulder, spreading contentment throughout her body.

"Okay?" Max asked.

"Oh, yes." She gazed at him in admiration. "You're very good with children, Max."

"Ah, it's easy with this bunch." He kissed Baby Peter's head, coming so near she could almost run her hands through his raven hair. He straightened, gave her yet another long, serious look, then added, "If you're okay, I'll check on Joseph and Emily."

"We're perfect."

Max sauntered out of the room and turned off the lamp, leaving Marilyn in semi-darkness. The baby whimpered, so she began to rock and hum. The nursery, with the help of a *Sesame Street* night-light, glowed with cheerfulness. Yellows, greens, and blues decorated the walls and the linens in the oak crib. Soft curtains framed the window, and a hand-braided rug covered the floor.

Baby Peter exhaled, his breath hot and moist against her neck. Marilyn closed her eyes, etching the details in her mind, and fighting off the envy that clawed at her. She craved exactly what Sondra had. Business. Love. Marriage. Children. From the moment she'd recognized her parents' apathy for each other *and* for her, she'd wished for a loving family on every falling star.

But she couldn't have it.

She'd learned the hard way that she was meant to live alone. First her parents, who'd never loved each other, left her to fend for herself. Next, after her mother died, her father treated her like an object to be discarded. She'd tried reaching out, but every time she did, she grabbed emptiness.

Finally, her fiancé dealt the final blow. Less than two years ago, as they discussed wedding plans, she'd revealed her secret. Six weeks later, he married another woman—a woman who could give him what she couldn't.

Baby Peter shifted and Marilyn checked his eyes. They were closed and his mouth pursed in an almost-kiss. She caressed his velvet-smooth cheek, and fought to ignore the ache in her heart. She had to savor this opportunity to hold a child, to cuddle and soothe a baby. Because, due to a medical condition discovered during her late teens, Marilyn could never have the one thing in life she desired most.

She couldn't have children.

Chapter Three

What seemed like seconds later, Marilyn opened her eyes, and saw a tall man in a gray suit standing over her.

She flinched, hugging Baby Peter closer. *Gerald?*

"Well, look who made a new friend," the man whispered.

"Peter?" She blinked, glad she hadn't spoken out loud. "What happened?"

"You fell asleep with your new buddy," Peter said. "Here, let me take him."

He gently laid his son in the crib, then walked into the hallway. Marilyn followed. After all these years, she still couldn't believe Peter and Max were brothers. Peter favored his mother. He had sandy hair, blue eyes, and aristocratic features. Max, like Hannibal, was dark and sharp-edged.

She stifled a yawn. "What time is it?"

"About ten. Sondra and I swung by the hospital to see Pop. Hope you don't mind."

"No, not at all. How's he doing?"

"Good. Your visit cheered him up."

"I'm glad. Thank you."

Peter was such a nice man. Marilyn sighed with painful memories. Her ex-fiancé, Gerald Kurtz, had been very much like Peter—handsome, well-dressed, and successful. Too bad he'd lacked a loving heart.

"Where is Sondra?" she asked, shoving the past into the back of her mind where it belonged.

"She's checking on Emily and Joseph. Oh, Max said he'd see you early in the morning to check the exterior."

She arched an eyebrow. "He's not here?"

"He left a couple of minutes ago," he said. "I found him stretched out on the sofa holding the baby monitor."

Baby monitor? Marilyn cringed inwardly. Had she heard her rusty attempts at singing? "He fell asleep?" she asked hopefully.

"As usual. Max is an early-to bed, early-to-rise type of guy. He's a great example for the kids." Peter grinned. "You know, get lots of sleep and grow big and strong like Uncle Max."

I'm convinced.

"I guess we're not the best of baby-sitters," she said, "falling asleep like that."

"Are you kidding? You're great. Kitchen and bathroom clean, the kids in bed. Perfect."

Sondra stepped out of Joseph's room. "Who's perfect?"

"Marilyn and Max."

"Oh?" She waggled her eyebrows. "Just what went on between my baby-sitters?"

"We baby-sat," Marilyn said, stalling a blush. "How's

the restaurant doing? I haven't been there in a couple of years."

"Business is booming. Come on. I'll give you a ride home and tell you all about it."

Once in the car, Marilyn made sure to keep the subject off her and Max. Everyone knew she'd had a crush on him, but no one, not even Sondra, knew Marilyn had done anything about it.

"I'm glad Sondra's Wild West Saloon is doing well," she said as they turned out of Sondra's subdivision. "On Connorsville's Main Street, Dodge-City–style buildings are popular, aren't they?"

"The Old West packs 'em in."

"I'm jealous," Marilyn confessed. "I've always wanted my own company and here you've done it."

"Isn't that what you plan to do with the money you get from the house?"

"Yes."

"So, sign the contract with Max and get started."

"That's what Hannibal said."

"Lynnie, I said I wouldn't pressure you, but you've got to understand the situation. The same people that have increased my business are building houses—quickly. To keep up, Max has stretched Connors and Son to the limit." She stopped at a light and let out a long breath. "Now with Pop out of the picture—"

"Out of the picture?" Anxiety flustered Marilyn. "Wh-what do you mean, out of the picture?"

"Complications from the heart attack. High blood pressure." She reached for a tissue and wiped her eyes. "Dr. Randalls told him he couldn't handle any more stress. Pop has to retire."

"Oh no." Marilyn clutched a hand to her throat, but clarity brightened her mind. "Poor Hannibal. Now I understand why he's worried about Max dying alone."

"What?"

"He said Max wasn't looking for a wife because of Brittany." She paused, uncertain she wanted to know the answer, then asked, "But who is she?"

"No one worth knowing," Sondra spat out. "The witch."

"Sondra!" The condemnation in her friend's voice surprised her. Sondra liked everyone. "For goodness sake, who is she?"

"An upwardly mobile architect who left Max back on the drawing board." Sondra paused. "It happened about six years ago, right before Angela Connors died. Brittany and Max talked about marriage, but she hated it here. She constantly badgered Max to leave, to move up in the world. All Peter and I know is, soon after their mother's funeral, Brittany left."

"Foolish woman."

"I say good riddance."

"I mean any woman who doesn't see how important the Connorses are to Connorsville and vice versa is an idiot."

"You got my vote, girlfriend." Sondra sighed. "Max hasn't been the same since."

Marilyn's heart reached out to Max. Rejection hurt. She knew all about that.

Then her mind flashed back to Brittany's phone call. Max had acted annoyed, not hurt or upset. "He seems okay to me," she said. "Maybe you worry too much."

Sondra pulled up in front of Aunt Phoebe's house and turned off the engine. "Maybe. But Lynnie, you saw how great he is with the kids. He's father material through and through. He ought to be spawning the next generation of master carpenters instead of burying himself in work."

"Does he do that?"

"You sign the contract and just watch him."

Marilyn paused to look up at the house, the only place she'd ever been happy. "I'll think about it. Thanks for the ride."

"Thank *you* for cleaning up my kitchen. Now I can go home and smooch with my husband instead of doing dishes." She laughed. "Good night, Lynnie. Call me if you get lonely."

Marilyn climbed out of the car and swallowed her envy. *If* she got lonely? She'd been lonely all her life.

She shook off the wallowing-weasel act and climbed the porch steps. Her thoughts immediately turned to Max. She couldn't envision him losing at love. He had everything going for him. Why had Brittany left? What had kept Max from going after her? And why, when she'd called tonight, hadn't she spoken to him?

Marilyn strolled inside and up the stairs to bed, but those questions, and knowing he'd be around first thing in the morning, kept her awake for a long time. She eventually abandoned sleep altogether and started going through her aunt's things.

She started in her favorite room—the kitchen.

The next morning, Max climbed onto Marilyn's roof. A cool, after-the-storm wind whipped his jacket against his body, and the wooden shingles poked his backside. He took a deep breath, peered out over his hometown, and started his count. "Five, ten, fifteen . . ." He stopped when he reached fifty, pride in the number of homes built by his family warming him against the chill. He turned as the sun peeked over the horizon, and brilliant shades of orange, red, and yellow bathed Connorsville in a fiery glow.

Bathed. The image of Marilyn shampooing Emily's hair filled his mind. Confusion immediately set in. She'd been dressed to the nines, career woman all the way. Yet she'd kicked off her shoes and rolled up her sleeves, without covering her expensive skirt and blouse. And a soft glow had flushed her face. That glow, and her subsequent look of panic when he'd mentioned her having babies, had danced in his mind all night.

A yawn shook him and he stretched.

Marilyn was a picture of contrasts. First, she'd looked stricken at the mention of children, then proved a champ at handling them. Then she'd seemed anxious to get away, yet sat and rocked Baby Peter until he'd quieted. Max sighed. He could still hear her soft voice humming and cooing. The moment he'd picked up the baby monitor, he'd been entranced.

Her soothing voice had lulled him, relaxed him until he couldn't keep his eyes open. Then Pete had caught him asleep, with the monitor clutched to his chest, and Max had been eager to leave. Having warm fuzzies for a woman who had no intention of sticking around would only lead to disappointment. So he'd left without even telling her good night.

This morning, though, he had to put aside his feelings—whatever they were—and finish his inspection of Marilyn's house. He'd promised Pop to convince her to restore the entire place, and Max never broke a promise.

A voice called out from below. "Are you out of your mind?"

He glanced down to see Marilyn standing on her front porch. He was instantly transported back to the first summer he'd seen her. He'd been on a roof then, too, hammering shingles in the hot Texas sun. She'd been fourteen and a general pest.

Now she stood in a sky-blue bathrobe, the belt loosely tied. He could see the embroidered neckline of her pink nightshirt. He swallowed. She definitely didn't look fourteen anymore.

Nor did she look like a cold career woman.

"At least I have all my clothes on," he called.

His voice echoed in the calm morning. From thirty feet up he saw her wince, but she didn't move.

"I'm properly dressed for pre-dawn," she said. "What are you doing up there?"

He stared at her. "Properly dressed? In that?"

A truck rounded the corner. She jumped, pulled the robe closer, and tightened the belt. Shading her eyes, she peered up at him again. "If I promise to change, will you come down?"

"No. I've got to check the shingles."

The pickup drew closer and Marilyn turned sharply. Max watched her dash into the house, then took a calming breath and returned to his inspection.

The cedar shingles looked good. The gutters along the roof were clear of debris and well-attached. He moved around the chimney to examine the flashing, then Marilyn leaned out a window near him and whispered angrily, "Did you have to shout? You'll wake the whole neighborhood."

"Afraid of a little gossip?" he asked. "Don't worry, Marilyn, nobody's going to spread rumors behind your back. Not with me sitting up here."

"Don't you get it? You're the one *causing* the rumors."

Max paused. She'd thrown on some clothes, but her

hair was still tousled from sleep. He'd never seen anyone look so good so early in the morning.

"Me? Marilyn, I spend my life on rooftops. Believe me, no one will think anything about it."

She started to speak, but an elderly woman yelled from the house across the street. "Maximilian Connors, what are you doing?"

"Morning, Mrs. Alford." Max waved and smiled. "Just checking Marilyn's roof."

The older woman shook her head. "Well, do it more quietly. Your voice booms like cannons on the Fourth of July."

"Yes, ma'am. Sorry to have bothered you."

Marilyn withdrew, then stuck her head out again. "Will you come off the roof if I brew some coffee—freshly ground from Mocha Heaven?"

"That wimpy stuff?" He frowned. "No thanks."

"Don't tell me you're one of *those*," she said, rolling her eyes.

Max quirked an eyebrow. "Those?"

"Yeah, those," she repeated, shuddering in mock horror. "Those thick-as-sludge coffee drinkers."

"Nah, that's wimpy stuff, too."

"You don't mean . . ." She clamped a hand over her mouth then spread her fingers ever so slightly. "So strong it stands by itself—no cup required?"

He grinned. "Now you've got it."

"I see. How about I toss you a few beans and you chew on them?" she quipped.

"Just add enough hot water so the beans clump together."

She laughed. A sweet, lilting laugh that floated on the morning air. Max laughed, too, the exchange warming his heart. Imagine, Marilyn with a sense of humor! Incredible.

"Okay, okay, I give up," she said, raising her hands in surrender. "I'll get out the cast-iron pot and start boiling the water. *Now* will you vacate your rooftop perch?"

"I'll be down in twenty minutes."

"*Quietly?*"

He chuckled. "Like a rusty chain saw."

"Oh, lucky me."

Rolling her eyes again, she pulled her head back inside the house and closed the window, but Max didn't move. Had he really heard her laughing and joking? She'd been too shy to say boo when she'd been a teenager. Now she seemed too distant.

"More contrasts," he muttered, more confused than ever. Thank goodness he had work to clear his head.

He made a few more notes, backed down the ladder, and jumped to the ground with a thump. He grinned. Inspecting houses was like a being a kid again, except he scrambled over rooftops instead of climbing up trees. An examination of the wood siding and the foundation came next, then—Suddenly his nose caught the aroma of fresh coffee, and he hurried to the back door.

Through the window, he could see Marilyn moving around the kitchen. She'd piled her hair on her head, exposing a long, graceful neck. She pulled something out of the oven and set it on a rack to cool. He reached for the handle to open the door, but she pressed the towel to her face.

He stopped, startled. Her shoulders shook and he realized she was crying. Protectiveness surged through him, and he wanted to hurry inside and comfort her.

He couldn't, shouldn't do that, though. He didn't know her very well, and . . . Dang it, he couldn't stand to see a woman cry, but he had to stay outside. Going inside would mean getting close, getting personal. He couldn't get personal with Marilyn. They were about to embark on a working relationship.

Since she was determined to get back to Chicago and he was determined never to leave Connorsville, a working relationship was the only kind they could have.

If he held her, he'd want more.

Max moved away from the window and rapped lightly on the door. "Hey, Marilyn," he yelled, as if he'd just come down off the roof, "do I smell coffee?"

He heard the clatter of baking pans and the shuffling of feet. Or was that sniffling? After a few moments, she opened the door, her expression completely neutral. "You certainly do. Come in."

"Thanks." He passed next to her, noting her eyes held no tears, but her nose was red.

"You finished pretty quickly," she said, a slight hitch in her voice. "Everything okay?"

"That's what I'd like to talk to you about."

A haunted look came into her eyes and she backed up. "Of course." She took the tray she'd removed from the oven, and held it between them like a barrier. "Cinnamon roll?"

The scent of fresh pastry wafted across his nose, and his mouth watered, but he shook his head. He had to get down to business. "Coffee's fine."

"Are you sure?" She handed him a mug, her hands a little shaky. "I couldn't sleep last night, so I started going through Aunt Phoebe's recipe box. She'd marked these as prizewinners."

"Couldn't sleep? Why?"

She turned to stare out the window over the sink, obviously lost in thought. "It's difficult without Aunt Phoebe here. My head is so full of memories."

"Right." Max mentally kicked himself for forgetting her grief, and at the same time was a bit surprised. Though she'd mentioned the cookies and lemonade she'd made with her aunt, he'd assumed they hadn't been close. Now he wasn't sure.

About anything.

"Max, I want to do what's right with this house."

"Then restore it," he said, glad to be back to business. "What could be better than that?"

She sank onto a kitchen chair and rested her chin in her palm. "I don't know. I wish Aunt Phoebe were here so I could ask her what she wants." Tears shimmered in her eyes. "But if she were, I wouldn't have to ask, would I?"

Max didn't know what to say. He'd grieved for his mother for months, missing her wisdom, wishing he'd said and done more for her while she was alive. He'd worked through his sorrow, but didn't have a clue how to tell someone else to do it.

"Maybe," he said haltingly, "you should wait a couple of days before you decide about the house."

She looked up at him, her eyes pleading. "You think so?"

He took a deep breath and nodded, shrugging off his frustration. It would cost him to advise her to wait. A postponement could delay his future, and that of Connors and Son. Yet her sadness tore at him. He couldn't take advantage of her grief.

"Marilyn," he said, "I need to be straight with you."

She got up to pour herself some coffee, then returned to the table, and indicated he join her. "And I need some advice."

He sat, then raised an eyebrow. "From me?"

"I'd prefer a disinterested third party," she said, "but you'll do."

"Okay," he said, shifting in his seat. "Shoot."

She stared at her feet, at the ceiling, everywhere but him. Her nervousness made him nervous.

"Here's the situation—a hypothetical situation."

He nodded. "Hypothetical."

"Woman has beautiful old home to redo. Option One is do the job fast and cheap."

"Which means you get back to your job on time with your finances intact."

"Exactly."

"Option One is your obvious choice."

Distress clouded her gray eyes. "But what if Option Two, to restore it back to its original glory, is what my aunt would really want?"

"You think that's why she left it to you?"

"I don't know it in my head, but I feel it in my heart."

"But Option Two will take longer." He paused, trying not to be selfish and demand she take the second option—hire him to renovate the house. "And you can't be sure what you'll find once you get started. The cost could break you."

"But Aunt Phoebe loved this house."

Max held his breath. Could Marilyn have loved her aunt, really had a family connection? Enough to delay returning to her job and do the house correctly? He wanted to believe it. He also knew why he wanted to believe it, because believing it meant he'd get the job.

So he didn't say anything. Just nodded.

"Then again, time *is* money," she said, "and I could benefit from a quick sale."

Max groaned inwardly. "Tough decision."

He'd lost. He could see it in Marilyn's eyes. She wanted out of Connorsville, and a quick fix would take less than a month. Restoration, on the other hand, would probably take the whole summer, maybe longer. He felt his future slipping through his fingers, but what could he do?

"Go with the quick fix," he said finally. "Take care of the items a home inspector would deem necessary, and put it up for sale."

"Thank you, Max," she said. "I knew I could rely on your integrity."

Integrity? He shook his head. His integrity had just talked him out of a lucrative contract. Still, he had to be honest. And being honest meant giving her all the facts. "At the risk of losing some of it, can I say one last thing?"

"Certainly."

"Restoring your house is a big opportunity for Connors and Son. If it will help, I won't charge you for my time." He laid a hand on her arm. "I can't do anything about the subcontractors, but I'll give you a discount on the carpentry and materials."

Her bare arm felt cool and soft in his hand. A zing of attraction raced through his fingers and he hesitated. Maybe he was shooting himself in the foot by pushing for restoration. He didn't want to be attracted to her, or any woman. Attraction led to love, which led to broken promises and painful rejection. He didn't want to travel that road again.

She looked first at his hand, then at his face. "Max, why would you do that for me?"

"Because you're a friend of the family. Because your aunt was a pillar of the community." He released her and crossed his arms over his chest. "But mostly because this house could be my stepping stone into the future."

Her eyes narrowed and she pushed to her feet. "I see. All for the glory of Connors and Son Construction."

He stood, too. "Yeah."

"I appreciate your honesty, Max." She backed up, and turned to the window. "I'll let you know."

Max left his written estimate on the table, then strode out the front door, chiding himself. He'd pushed too hard. She was upset and he'd stepped on her toes. Any of the builders in town could do the fix-up work. Not only had he lost the restoration contract, he'd probably lost the chance to set foot in the house again. Now what would Connors and Son do?

He shook his head and climbed into his pickup. No way would he be the generation to ruin the family business. Four generations of Connors and Son depended on him and he would *not* let them down. Determined, he shoved the truck in gear and headed for work. Maybe a brilliant solution would strike him on the way to the construction site. With Pop out of commission, and the six custom homes behind schedule, nothing short of a miracle would do.

Marilyn waited for the roar of Max's truck, then slowly moved to look at the estimate. His earthy scent drifted up from the paper, warming her, making her wish she could stay in Connorsville just to get to know Max better.

But she couldn't.

Instead, she chewed her lip and focused on the figures. Her jaw dropped at the bottom line. She had more than enough money for a quick fix. What had she been worried about?

She pushed the paper away. "I'm sorry, Aunt Phoebe," she said to the air. "I know you loved this house. I want to make it beautiful again, but I can't work with Max every day."

She swiped at a tear. The phone rang and she jumped. It wasn't even 8:00 yet. Who'd call this early? Was it bad news? She snatched the receiver off its hook.

"Lynnie?"

"Sondra?" Her breath caught. "Is it Hannibal? What's wrong?"

"Nothing. It's good news. I didn't mean to startle you. I've been up with Baby Peter for hours. I didn't realize . . ."

Marilyn's racing heart slowed. "It's okay. What's the good news?"

"They're moving Pop into a private room today. He's off those machines and breathing on his own."

Marilyn slumped against the wall. "Thank goodness."

"We're all relieved," Sondra said. "Thought you'd want to know."

"Yes. Thank you, Sondra. Thanks a lot."

Marilyn hung up, instantly angry with herself. She'd promised Hannibal if he took care of himself she'd talk with Max. How could she have gone against her promise so quickly? She hadn't talked with Max, she'd shut him out. No wonder he'd left in a huff.

She straightened, picked up the estimate, grabbed her cell phone, and punched in Max's number at the construction office.

"Connors and Son Construction," he said crisply.

She blinked. "You answer your own phone?"

"Marilyn? Trying to catch up on some paperwork. I hate computers."

She hesitated, not sure how to proceed. "Sondra just

called, said Hannibal is doing well enough to move out of intensive care."

"Yeah, great isn't it? Personally, I think the nurses got tired of his griping."

She laughed, then sobered remembering Hannibal saying having his two daughters home was the best medicine. She had to keep her promise. "Max, do you have a minute to walk through this estimate with me?"

"Well, I can't come now—"

"No, I mean I'll walk through the house while you talk. I'm on my cell phone." She paused. "I apologize for not doing this while you were here. I'm tired—"

"And I'm sorry for pushing so hard." His voice softened. "I know you miss your aunt."

Tears welled up in her eyes. She didn't want him to be kind. Gruff she could handle, but a considerate Max touched her heart. "Thank you. Shall we?"

For the next several minutes, Marilyn toured the farmhouse with Max's deep voice booming descriptions and explanations in her ear. She heard very little, but saw a lot. The front porch sagged on one end. Paint peeled off the dark green shutters and the yellow clapboards. The carriage house doors hung askew, and the driveway needed to be repaired and sealed.

Back inside, she started with the attic the way Max had when he had been with her. Cracks in the walls and ceilings needed patching and paint. The wood floors were scuffed, and a couple of windows had lost their screens, but everything worked—doors, windows, plumbing, etc.

"Inside is in better shape, isn't it?"

"Connors and Son build only the best," he said lightly.

"Yes, I can see that." And she could. She jumped up and down on the second floor landing and nothing moved, not the vase on the table in the corner, not the portrait of Aunt Phoebe's grandmother on the wall. The boards didn't even squeak.

She returned to the first floor and gazed up at the parlor ceiling. A mural of fluffy white clouds and golden cherubs gazed back. A wide walnut archway led into the dining room, where a cut-glass chandelier sparkled in the morning sun.

"I thought this was a farmhouse," she said.

"It's what we call a four-over-four. Two-story, central staircase, two rooms on either side," Max said. "But the original owner was a wealthy man. He built the standard house, added the third floor, a back staircase, and attached the kitchen to the rear instead of keeping it a separate building."

"Is that why the back porch is shaped like a question mark?"

He chuckled. "Yeah, they had to work around the addition. Can't have a Victorian without a kitchen porch. It's like cake without icing."

"And your great-grandfather did it all?"

"Yeah," he said, pride evident in his voice. "Thus began Connors and Son Construction."

"This was his first house?"

"As a builder, yeah. I live in the first house he built, but that was a matter of—"

"Pleasing his bride," she finished for him. Yes, she knew the story and envy struck her like a hammer. Max had so much history. Everywhere he looked something of him or his family lived on. Once she sold this house, she'd have nothing. No family, no children, no legacy.

She had to get out of here and get back to Chicago where the memories didn't stare her in the face. "When can you start?" she asked.

"Are you kidding?"

"The basics, Max. I only have three weeks from my job."

There was silence and Marilyn shook the phone, wondering if she'd lost the connection. Then his voice rumbled again. "How about tomorrow morning?"

"Before dawn?" she asked lightly.

"Has to be. I won't lie to you, Marilyn, I'll be running back and forth between your house and the subdivision until I get back on schedule. It'll be hit and miss for a while. If you want to hire someone else, I'll understand."

First he was kind, now he was being noble. She chewed her lip. "I don't want to hire anyone else."

His voice lifted. "Great. See you in the morning, and I'll try not to get there before seven."

"Thank you. I'll go into the kitchen right now and start clumping coffee beans."

He laughed out loud, and her heart warmed to the sound. "Thanks, Marilyn, you've made my day."

Max and his crew flowed in and out of Marilyn's house for the next several days, beginning at 7:00 and quitting at sundown, unless the standard 5:00 Texas thunderstorm broke into the routine. As May flowed into June, Marilyn learned that her bedroom was the quietest, and the most dust-free. So she set up her computer, rented a fax machine, and tried to do some work so she wouldn't be behind when she returned to Chicago.

"Marilyn?" Max called out late one afternoon. His voice boomed from the stairwell. "You up there?"

She sighed. Being on the second floor meant constant trips downstairs to talk with Max. She turned off her monitor and walked down the carpeted steps, following the sound of his voice.

"You'd make a great actor on the stage," she said when she found him in the parlor. "You don't need a microphone."

"I spend a lot of time yelling over machines."

"Of course. So, what did you need?"

He took her hand and drew her to the coffee table. Several yellowed and aged papers with lines and numbers lay before her. "Look what I found," he said.

"What?"

"The original blueprints. See?" His face beamed. "Remember I mentioned I didn't think the closet under the stairs was original? Well, I started digging through Great-Grandpa's old trunk and I found these."

She plopped next to him on the Victorian settee, aware of nothing but his warmth and the undeniable excitement in his dark eyes. They sparkled until they were almost brown instead of black.

"I want to repeat my offer, Marilyn," he said, tracing the lines on the blueprints. "This house could be a showplace, if you'd let me totally restore it." He paused and looked at her. "I'd bet the Connorsville Historical Society would add it to their annual tour."

She sat forward. "Aunt Phoebe mentioned that once. But you're talking more than minor repairs. Even with your discount, the cost could run into the thousands. I've toured houses in Chicago. They use hand-stenciled wallpaper, and specially mixed paint to recreate the original colors."

"It's worth a shot to check it out," he said. "You may even get a break on property taxes."

She searched his face. Bright smile, glowing eyes; he resembled a child at Christmas. "You enjoy your work, don't you?"

"Yeah. Let me show you." He took her hand and

pulled her over to the staircase. The carved newel post reflected the light flowing through the front door's leaded glass. He placed her palm on the carving. "Feel that?"

Rich, polished wood greeted her fingertips. "It's very smooth."

He placed his hand over hers, warming her skin and her heart. Not only did she love his touch, she loved his enthusiasm. Her job hadn't excited her that way in a long time, and she hoped starting her own agency would change all that.

"Feel it again," he said, his rough palm guiding her.

Minuscule bumps, nicks, and indentations in the varnished wood grazed her fingertips. She looked up in amazement. "But it looks so even."

"Chisel marks, sanded, polished, varnished to perfection." He pulled her hand away, but didn't release her. "You see how the wood has a richer, deeper color? That's character, a mark of quality workmanship."

Intrigued, and eager to get out of his reach, she moved to another section. Her eyes widened. "No nicks or dents at all."

"Replaced about fifteen years ago," he said. "Manufactured on an assembly line."

She stepped back, and like that first day, the foyer wrapped around her like a warm blanket, with Max generating the warmth. "This is what you want to do, isn't it? The detail work. Hand-carving, and all the rest."

"Yeah. I still have the old tools, and I'm good at it. I know restoring the entire house will take longer, but believe me, you'll enjoy the results for years to come."

Her enthusiasm fled. "No, I won't be around then. The new owners would have that privilege."

"Yeah, I forgot." His expression darkened. "You're eager to sell this place, aren't you?"

No. In a perfect world, Marilyn would stay right there and relive Aunt Phoebe's love for the rest of her life. But the world wasn't perfect, and remaining in Connorsville would torture her beyond belief.

"It's what I have to do, Max. For my career, for my independence."

"Right." He rubbed his jaw. "Well, think about restoration, will you?"

She pushed by him and ran up the stairs to her bedroom. She tried to work, but couldn't concentrate on résumés, personnel statistics, and human resources programs. So she walked up the next flight to the third floor attic.

It was a huge room with a finished floor and walls, obviously used for children or servants at some time. Boxes lined one side with odd tags and markings. On the other side sat some furniture—the antiques Max had mentioned. Aunt Phoebe's mother-in-law had passed on some pieces that Phoebe had apparently hated and stashed out of sight. Dust and cobwebs covered them, so Marilyn turned her attention to the boxes.

Below her, hammers pounded nails on the porch posts, and a saw buzzed, cutting lumber in the side yard. She blocked out the noise and began opening trunks.

The first of the three held books, letters, and old clothes, plus a few pressed flowers. The second held much the same. The third, however, scented with citrus potpourri and full to the brim, shocked and surprised Marilyn.

A note in the lid caught her attention. "The Marilyn Waters Scrapbook." Tears filled her eyes. Aunt Phoebe had saved her things? She pulled out boxes, photo albums, and recipe cards, dozens of them, all covered with the same scrapbook note.

When she pulled out a crayon recipe for chocolate-chip cookies, grief gripped Marilyn so hard she sank to the floor. Like a starved child, she delved into the trunks, hungry for each piece of paper, for each pressed flower. Sobs convulsed her body until her chest hurt and tears blurred her vision.

If only she'd known. Oh, if she'd only realized Aunt Phoebe truly loved her and missed her. If Marilyn had known, she would have visited more, called her more, been more open about her own feelings. Instead, she'd held them back, choosing to believe her father, who'd insisted Aunt Phoebe was merely doing him a favor, that she didn't care about Marilyn at all.

Marilyn swallowed. She was finished with her father's lies. Maybe she couldn't have done more while Aunt Phoebe was alive, but she could certainly do something now. She could restore the house and do it right like Max had suggested. He had the original plans, and the talent. All she needed was the money. She'd cash in some stocks, or use them to secure a loan. Whatever it took, she'd do it. For Aunt Phoebe.

A noise from the doorway startled her. "Marilyn, you okay?"

"Max?" She flushed and swiped at her tears. "Is something wrong?"

"Just what I was about to ask you." He crouched next to her. "Why are you crying?"

She couldn't speak, merely indicated the papers.

He held up a crude crayon drawing of a family; mother, father, a girl with yellow hair and an orange dog. "Refrigerator art," he said. "Joseph make you a 'picher'?"

She shook her head. He looked at the name at the

bottom. "Oh, you did this. Your aunt saved your stuff. My mom did that. I still have boxes and boxes."

"There are articles from Chicago newspapers, college graduation, the letter I wrote to the editor." Her voice scraped in her throat. "How did she get these here in Texas?"

"Maybe she subscribed by mail, or bought them at that big bookstore in Plano." He shrugged. "That's what families do."

In her experience, families ignored one another. Dear Aunt Phoebe. Renewed grief swamped Marilyn. "I miss her so much."

She began to sob again, and Max drew her into his arms. His body felt like a rock, like solid, dependable granite. She buried her face in his shirt and let the tears flow.

"Shhh." He stroked her hair. "I know it hurts. I won't say the pain goes away entirely, but it dulls." He sat and pulled her onto his lap like a child. "Give it time, Marilyn."

She relaxed. Who would have guessed loud, blustery Max could be so gentle? She'd seen it with Sondra's children; why hadn't she recognized him as more than a candidate for fatherhood, as a caring man? She hiccupped. "How much time, Max?" she asked softly. "First my mother, now my aunt."

He thumbed away her tears. "I can't tell you that," he said softly. "It took me a long time to get over my mother's death. I still miss her wisdom."

Compassion and sincerity warmed his dark eyes, and she felt safe, protected in his hold. Her tension eased and she reached up to stroke his face. "Thank you, Max."

He hugged her and dropped a kiss on her forehead. Warmth flooded her, along with memories of her eighteenth birthday. He'd done the same thing then, held her, treated her like a sweet child. She'd insisted on a grown-up kiss, but he'd shoved her away, insisting she run home like a good little girl and play with her dolls.

She'd been devastated.

What would he do now? She'd wondered about it for years. Why not kiss him again and see what happened? She blinked, angled her head, then raised her lips to meet his.

Chapter Four

Max accepted her invitation and kissed her lightly. To his surprise, she tasted sweet and fresh, not hard like he'd expected. He held her a moment longer, wanting to kiss her again, but like fifteen years ago, he couldn't. Then, she'd been too young and he'd pushed her away to protect her.

Those same protective feelings surged through him now. As a teenager, she'd always looked so lonely, in need of a friend. Now she looked as if she'd lost her whole world. He couldn't take advantage of her vulnerability. She could get hurt.

So could he.

He released her. He couldn't get involved with Marilyn. She was leaving. He was staying. It was that simple—and that difficult. Her eyes popped open.

"Max?"

He cleared his throat, and glanced around the room, searching for something to distract him from kissing her again.

"You could clean up those antiques," he said, his voice rough, "and put them downstairs. Attract a lot of buyers."

Pain clouded her stormy gray eyes. "Of course," she said. She pulled from his embrace, and struggled to stand. "Is that what you came up here for?"

"No." He stood and ran a hand over his jaw. He had no idea why he'd come into the attic. "I mean, yeah."

"In view of what just happened, I think it's better not to restore the house."

"Wait. Marilyn, don't give up on the house because of me. I got carried away." He reached for her. "I'm sor—"

"No, don't." She stepped back. "Don't apologize."

"Okay." Max took a deep breath to clear his head, and drew in her rose scent instead. He swallowed. "But I thought you wanted to do right by this house."

"I do." She indicated the memorabilia on the floor between them. "After seeing this, I realized Aunt Phoebe left me the house because she thought I'd do the right thing."

"So restore it." He scolded himself rapidly. He'd blown the deal—again. He'd let whatever was between them reopen old wounds. "I promise you—"

"I don't think either of us is in a position to make promises." She smoothed a honey-colored tendril behind her ear. "I can't afford to restore it, not like it should be done. So the best thing for me to do is fix it up, sell, and let the new owners give it the loving care it needs."

"Marilyn, I . . ."

"Please, Max, don't argue. It's better this way and we both know it."

"Fine." He crossed his arms, trying to quell his sense of defeat. "I'll push to crew to finish and get out of your hair."

"Good." With dignity, she marched past him and downstairs.

Max chewed himself out for days. He'd let his attraction for Marilyn get out of control. He'd made the same mistake when she was eighteen. Right here in this house, actually on the back porch, she'd kissed him. He'd expected an experimental, immature kiss, but her sweetness had touched him. He'd wanted to kiss her back, but had covered it up by pushing her away, claiming she was too young for him. Just a child.

Now he'd hurt her again, taken advantage of her grief and held her too close. He might be a master at carpentry, but when it came to understanding women, he was barely a novice.

To keep his mind off her, and the kiss, he dove into his work, dividing his time between Marilyn's fix-up, the other construction sites, and visiting his father in the hospital. At first, it was enough to distract him, then Hannibal returned home and the custom houses practically began building themselves.

"That's what I get for hiring such a good crew," Max said one hot June afternoon. Storm clouds gathered on the horizon, both inside and outside the house. Marilyn's scent, her tawny hair, which she wore up exposing her swanlike neck, and her quiet humming called to Max. She'd retreated to her computer in her second-floor bedroom, but he knew she was there.

He forced himself to concentrate. The casing around

the music room's sliding doors needed repair. Listening to the faint click-click of Marilyn's computer keys wouldn't help. Thank goodness an entire level separated them. At least he couldn't see her. The phone rang, like it did twenty times a day. Apparently, Marilyn was in demand.

He stopped hammering to listen.

"Yes?" he heard her say. "No, I'm stuck in Texas for a while longer."

Stuck? He frowned. He was stuck, not in Texas, but with her rose scent floating around his head. Why didn't the hot air carry her perfume up to the attic instead of down to him?

"Yes, I recommended her for the job," she said. "She's a perfect match."

Her voice deepened with emphasis, as if someone were giving her a hard time. Intrigued, Max moved to the foyer to listen better. He'd never heard Marilyn stand up for herself.

"Look at her credentials," she insisted. "She has the education, the experience."

Unable to resist, he quietly climbed the stairs till he reached the second floor landing.

"Examine the benefit package," Marilyn said into the phone. "It's substandard. That's why she's asking for a twenty-percent increase in salary."

He peeked into her room. She stood with her profile to him and he saw determination glint in her eyes. She started to pace, stopped, and glared out the window.

Max couldn't help himself; he leaned against the doorjamb and blatantly watched her. She wore shorts, emphasizing her trim legs, and a simple T-shirt, yet her attitude was as professional as that first day, when she'd been dressed in a suit.

"She's a single parent of four children, and two of them need braces," Marilyn continued. "One is about to enter college, the youngest plays sports."

She let go of the heavy floral drape and rolled her eyes. "*Medical* insurance. If the company paid a decent percentage, she wouldn't need to sock away half her increase for doctor bills." Marilyn covered the mouthpiece and muttered, "Idiot."

Max laughed. She swung around, her eyes wide, then crossed the room and shut the door in his face.

Caught off-guard—and almost without a nose—he stumbled, righting himself near the banister. Okay, he deserved that for eavesdropping. Better get back to work before he got something else slammed. Halfway to the landing, he paused, the edge in her voice halting him.

"Talk to them," she urged. "I'll bet you dinner at the restaurant of your choice she'll accept a lower salary if they beef up their package. No, I don't have another candidate waiting in the wings. This woman is *the* person for the job."

Max shook his head. This was a side of Marilyn he'd never seen—strong and confident. She obviously understood her clients' needs and fought for them.

He turned to go downstairs. The door behind him opened.

"Hasn't anyone ever told you eavesdropping is rude?" she asked.

"I couldn't help myself, you sounded . . ."

Her eyes blazed. "What? Angry? Frustrated?"

"A little of both. Problems?"

"Yes. No. Nothing I can't handle." She brushed a limp strand of hair from her forehead.

"Sounded like you made an impression, anyway."

"Does that surprise you?"

He relaxed against the banister. "Guess I'm used to thinking of you as a silent tag-along."

"Guess you don't know me very well then, do you?"

"Guess not."

But he'd like to. He moved closer. Her eyes widened. Then he remembered she'd be leaving in a few days. No point in being left behind again.

He backed up and ran a hand over his jaw. "Well, I guess I'll get back to work."

"Yes, do." Her face paled. "The sooner you finish, the sooner I can get back to Chicago."

He bristled. "Can't wait to leave?"

"My job's important to me."

"More important than anything else?"

"I *have* nothing else."

Her voice was flat, unemotional. Max grimaced. "What about this house? The history that goes with it? All the memories—"

"Max?" Hannibal's voice boomed from the foyer. "You here?"

Max excused himself and strode downstairs. "Pop, what are you doing here? You're supposed to be taking it easy."

"I've laid in that dang-blasted bed for three days now. It's so quiet I can hear my hair turning white." Outside, a saw whirred as the crew replaced part of the porch railing. Hannibal turned to the sound. "Ah, the buzz of work. Music to my ears." He faced Max again. "How's it going?"

"Hannibal?" Marilyn ran downstairs and hugged him. "What are you doing here? Are you all right?" She glanced up. "Max, should he be here?"

Max's gaze locked with hers. Concern filled her face. How could she say she didn't have anything here? What about Sondra, the kids, his father? Didn't they count? He held his breath to keep her scent from fogging his mind and whittling away his self-control. "No," he said. "But I could use his opinion."

Hannibal's face lit up. "Need the old man's expertise?"

"The staircase molding. Can't match the wood."

"The piece that was machine-done?" Marilyn interjected.

"How'd you know that?" Hannibal asked.

She blushed, and again her gaze locked with Max's. "Max pointed it out to me."

Max frowned. Contrasts again. A moment ago, she was almost cold. Now, her face was alive with emotion. She intrigued him, and frustrated him. What went on in her mind?

He shook his head. He did *not* care. He wasn't interested in Marilyn, or in any woman who put her career before family.

Hannibal arched an eyebrow. "Oh, he did, huh?"

"Come on, Pop," Max said. "Marilyn has work to do."

She glanced up the stairs, then frowned. "I think I'll take a break and make some iced tea." She kissed Hannibal's cheek, then hurried to the kitchen.

Max took his father through the house. Together, they marveled at their ancestor's handiwork.

"Does my heart good to be here," Hannibal said. He closed his eyes and took a deep breath. "Just smell that quality."

Max grinned. "That's construction dust."

"Not nearly enough of it. Why aren't you farther along?"

"We'll be done in four more days."

"Restoring the whole house?" Hannibal shook his head. "Not on your life."

Max sighed. He hadn't broken the news to Pop because he hadn't wanted to worry him, but he couldn't lie. "Marilyn's doing a quick fix-up."

Hannibal frowned. "But you found Grandpa's original plans."

"Bottom line. She can't afford it."

His father's face reddened. "It was your job to make it affordable. What happened?"

"Now, don't upset yourself." Max related the deal he'd made, discounting materials and time. "Can't go any lower."

"We'll see about that." Before Max could stop him, Hannibal took off toward the kitchen. "Marilyn? Darlin', where are you?"

"Pop, go home and relax," Max said, following. "Let me handle this."

"Marilyn!" Hannibal boomed again.

She appeared in the kitchen doorway, wringing a striped towel. "What's wrong? Did something happen?"

Hannibal halted in front of her. "You broke a promise, that's what's wrong."

She paled. Max arched an eyebrow. What kind of deal had she made with his father?

"No, I didn't." She straightened. "I talked to him."

Hannibal whirled to face Max. "So it's your fault."

"I have no idea what you're talking about. Besides, I told you the deal I made her."

"It obviously wasn't up to scratch."

"Hannibal, please," Marilyn said. "It's not Max's fault."

"Humph. One of you is to blame." His voice rose with

each word, and his face got redder. "This was a perfectly workable deal. So, get together and *work* it out."

Max laid a hand on his father's shoulder. "Okay, Pop. Don't stress out."

Marilyn moved forward, her soft gray eyes wide with alarm.

"Hannibal, please, don't excite yourself."

He relaxed, then winked at Max. "Her voice sounds like running molasses, doesn't it?"

Max paused, remembering how her voice had soothed him to sleep at Pete's when they were baby-sitting, but he wasn't going to admit that to Pop. Instead, he rolled his eyes. "Have you been taking your medication?"

"Keep your shirt on, I'm leaving." Hannibal frowned. "But I expect a full report tonight."

Max followed him to the door where they met Mrs. Alford, who looked as if she'd just come from the beauty parlor.

"Why, Betty," Hannibal said. "What are you doing here?"

"I could ask you the same thing, Hannibal Connors. Sakes alive, it's easy to tell where Max got his big voice. I heard you all the way across the street and over my television, too."

Hannibal looked contrite. "Sorry. I'll keep it down."

"Come in, please," Marilyn said. "Care for some iced tea?"

The older woman blushed slightly, and patted her gray hair. "Well, thank you, dear, but I really wanted to talk to the menfolk. I don't mean to bother you, but since you're working in the neighborhood." She paused again. "Well, I have this lose board on my porch."

Hannibal's face lit up. "Don't let it worry you another

second. Just show me where and I'll fix it in a jiffy. Can't have you falling and busting something."

Before Max had a chance to reply, his father had taken Mrs. Alford's elbow and ushered her down the walk.

Marilyn giggled.

"What's so funny?" Max asked.

"I think Mrs. Alford's sweet on your dad."

"Don't be silly."

"Look for yourself."

He joined her and peered through the old-fashioned screen door. Betty Alford held onto Pop's arm with one hand, and gestured nervously with the other.

Marilyn moved next to Max, brushing his shoulder. He inched aside. "You're seeing things," he said.

"No, I recognize the first blush of love when I see it. Don't you?"

She gazed up at him, her eyes silvery bright. He sucked air. He didn't want to read love in anyone's expression, ever again. It hurt too much when it ended.

"I don't see it," he insisted. "But love's never been my area of expertise." Then he strode back to the music room to finish the molding and get Marilyn on her way home.

Love was never his expertise?

Marilyn shook her head. Then they had something in common. She'd tried to gain her parents' love and failed. Romantic love had been a wash-out, too. Love of career was all she had left, and that wasn't faring too well.

Still, Max's reaction puzzled her. She knew he'd been hurt, but why deny his father companionship? Or even love? If anyone deserved to be happy, it was Hannibal. He'd been devoted to his wife, been a good husband and father. Why should he suffer through his retirement alone?

For the next three afternoons, Hannibal stopped in to give Max advice, and to hang around the work site. And every afternoon, Mrs. Alford required a minor repair that she'd completely forgotten about the day before.

Max watched the older couple with raised eyebrows. He watched Marilyn, too. She could feel his gaze on her, but didn't understand the look in his dark eyes. She should talk to him. Half the phone calls she'd received had been about the work being done on the house. The planning commission, the local historical society, and the county museum had called to answer *and* ask questions.

Rumor had obviously spread that she intended to renovate the house, and they wanted more information. She'd stalled them, no longer certain her decision for a quick fix was the right one. Her funds would easily cover the repairs, but her bank account had its limits. Restoration took time. If she stayed beyond her paid vacation, she could lose her job.

And risk losing her heart to Max all over again.

She didn't know what to do. Had her attraction for Max clouded her common sense? On the fourth day, after Hannibal again strolled arm in arm with Mrs. Alford over to her house for an afternoon of companionship, Marilyn joined Max at the front door.

"Think of it this way, Max," she said to him, struggling to think of a way to lighten his dark mood. "Helping Mrs. Alford makes your father feel useful."

"What does that mean?"

"He has to avoid stress, right?" she said.

"Yeah."

She gazed up into Max's dark eyes. They were distant and cold, unlike his normal self. "What's wrong with using his skills to help a neighbor and have a little conversation, too?"

"Nothing. Everything. I don't know, it just doesn't feel right." He turned to her. "We'll be done in another day or two, a full week ahead of your deadline. Ready to head home?"

"Home?"

Home was a house with love and security. She lived in a sparsely furnished apartment—alone.

"Thought your job was important to you," he said when she didn't elaborate.

"It is, or at least it will be when I start my own agency."

"You're starting your own business?" He arched an ebony eyebrow. "Why didn't you say so before? I understand what it takes to get a business off the ground."

"How? You were born into yours."

"I was born into a small family operation that builds, if we're lucky, ten homes a year." He paused. "Connorsville is growing and attracting people from Dallas, including builders who can put up twice that in half the time. For Connors and Son to compete we have to broaden our horizons."

"I didn't realize." Marilyn chewed her lip, remembering Sondra had said something like that. Why hadn't it registered then? She gave herself a mental reprimand. *Because you were too wrapped up in who Brittany was to pay attention.* "I'm sorry, Max, but even if I cashed in some stock, I can't afford it."

"Tough break."

She took a deep breath. "Yes, tough break."

The timer on the stove buzzed and she hurried into the kitchen. To her surprise, Max followed. "Have you abandoned your computer?" he asked.

"Too hot upstairs." She pulled a tray of low-fat chocolate-chip cookies from the oven. "Besides, I found some more of Aunt Phoebe's recipes."

She examined each cookie and found them evenly browned. Her mind flashed back to her aunt instructing her to make the most efficient use of all her ingredients, including the manner in which she spooned the dough onto the baking sheet.

"How do you do that?" he asked.

She glanced up. "Do what?"

"Get them to all come out the same size?"

She grinned, delighted. "Family secret."

Family. Sorrow gripped her and she set down the cookies to gaze out the window. Her aunt's flowers bloomed full and large. Red geraniums, yellow marigolds, and purple petunias fluttered in the hot breeze, their petals daring the Texas sun to wilt them.

Well, she couldn't wilt either. Aunt Phoebe had entrusted the house to her to be loved and cared for, not to be sold willy-nilly to the first buyer. She chewed her lip. "How much to really restore the house?"

"Thought you couldn't afford it."

"I'm not sure I can. I've seen home improvement shows on television, and the renovations usually run over cost." She paused. "You never know what's behind the walls until you open them up, right?"

"Generally, that's true." His eyes brightened, and a smile curved his lips. "That's the great thing about this particular house. My family built it. It's taken a few hits over the years, earned a few patch jobs, but since I have the original plans, I understand the changes. I'd bet, beyond code problems and modern conveniences, that this old beauty's not hiding much."

Still not convinced, she indicated the countertop and

the painted cabinets. "What about this World War Two kitchen?" she asked. "It's not even close to original."

"The floor is," he said, indicating the black-and-white hexagonal-shaped tiles. "The wiring's up to code, with the exception of the stove which can be put on a separate breaker. The cabinets and countertops are cosmetic changes."

"So how long do you think it would take?"

His eyes dulled and he frowned. "Paint has to be scraped. Some of it may even be lead-based, which means extra precautions and extra time. Wallpaper steamed off in bits and pieces. You want to take care not to damage the original woodwork, walls, and flooring. That means everything's done by hand."

"How long?"

"The whole summer, maybe longer."

She blew out a breath. Okay, she'd fulfilled her promise to Hannibal and talked to Max. She couldn't be away from her job that long. Even if she worked from here, she risked losing clients—important people she intended to take with her when she opened her own recruiting agency.

"What will Hannibal do now?" she asked, straining to keep her sanity and be true to Aunt Phoebe's memory, too.

Max frowned. "That's a good question. He's worked all his life. Staying at home will drive him nuts, but I can't let him get involved with work. Summer is Connors and Son's busiest and most stressful time. Long hours and lots of paperwork."

"Paperwork?" An idea sizzled in her mind like bacon on a griddle. "Did you say paperwork? Like invoices and supply orders, that sort of thing?"

"Yeah, why?"

Okay, this is it. The lights are on and everyone's home. This idea has to work.

Mentally crossing her fingers, Marilyn took a deep breath and said, "Do it. Restore this house as if it were your own."

"What?" He stared at her. "How? You just said . . ."

"I have a business degree, Max. What I can't pay in cold, hard cash, I'll trade in cold, hard figures."

"Excuse me?"

"Paperwork is my life, Max. I can fill out forms in my sleep and I'm a whiz at computers."

"Hmm," he said, rubbing a hand over his jaw. "You mean, scratch my back and I scratch yours?"

"Exactly. Like the old-fashioned barter system. You fix up my house, I straighten up your files."

He crossed his arms. "Why?"

"Because it's right." Tears filled her eyes. "Who loved this house more than my aunt?"

"No one."

She faced him. "And who loved my aunt more than me?"

He stared at her, obviously surprised by the question. "No one?" he asked gently.

"No one," she said. "That's a pure fact. So it's up to me to do what she wanted, and I believe she wanted me to stay and make sure her home looked its best."

He moved toward her. "What about your job, your own agency, Marilyn? I can't guarantee three months will do it."

"Remember when I said I wish I knew what my aunt wanted?"

He nodded. "You had a hard time making a decision."

"That's right, and in my experience, the tougher the decision, the harder you hit it. Straight on, no hesitation."

"Your experience?"

"Absolutely." With each word, she felt more confident, more certain she was doing the right thing. That she and Max could work together—just work. "Set it up. Start wherever you want. Do it right, and I'll help in any way I can."

He closed the gap between them, confusion clouding his strong features. "Marilyn, why are you doing this?"

"Because." She paused, seeking a way to explain, then remembered his words when he'd offered her the cut-rate deal on his time. "You're a friend of my aunt's family. The Connorses are pillars of the community. But mostly because Aunt Phoebe loved this house, and I loved her."

"You're sure? Once we begin, stopping will be difficult."

"I'm positive."

She marveled at her own certainty, but no doubt remained. The tension between her shoulder blades relaxed, the loneliness ebbed, and for the first time in weeks, her grief eased. She knew it was what her beloved Aunt Phoebe truly wanted.

"Then you've got a deal," he said.

Max held out his hand. She took it. His work-roughened palm skimmed hers, and the texture of his skin brought home exactly what she'd done to herself.

Instead of taking the chance to escape to Chicago, she'd agreed to face Max every day for the next three months. From early morning until late at night, she'd watch him, hear his voice, be drawn to his protective strength. She couldn't hide from him, because there would be consultations, questions to be answered, and his paperwork.

She groaned inwardly. How would she survive with her heart intact?

Chapter Five

What she'd done to herself became even more apparent the next morning. Hannibal appeared on her doorstep before sunrise. He grinned, hugged her, then indicated several people on the porch behind him. "Got a few friends for you to meet," he said.

Several professional-looking people strolled into the house, shook her hand, and starting making notes on paper-lined clipboards.

"Hannibal?" she asked. "What's going on?"

"Word travels fast," a man in paint-splattered coveralls said.

A woman dressed in designer clothes sighed. "I've been dying to do this house."

"Promised your aunt I'd redo that powder room at cost," a man in a khaki uniform added.

Marilyn stepped back and ran a hand through her tousled hair. "I'm sorry," she said. "I haven't had coffee yet. I'm a little muddled."

"Good morning, everyone," Max said as he crossed the threshold. "Have trouble finding the place?"

The crowd laughed, except Marilyn. "Max, what's going on?"

"Pop didn't tell you?"

"Sorry, darlin'," Hannibal said. "Thought I'd let it be a surprise."

"Let what be a surprise?"

Max spread his arms wide. "Them."

The woman stepped forward. "Ms. Waters, we've all worked for and with Connors and Son for years. We're willing to give you a deal on the restoration."

Marilyn arched an eyebrow. "In return for what?"

"You really didn't tell her," Max said, frowning. "Did you, Pop?"

Hannibal shrugged. "I'm old. I forget things."

Max rolled his eyes, and drew Marilyn out of the foyer into the music room. She couldn't take her eyes off him. He wore a T-shirt and jeans, like he had for the last few days, but she could have sworn she was fourteen again and gazing up at a Greek god. Her heart skittered.

"These people are willing to give you a similar deal to what I'm doing," he said.

An image of being buried under tons of paper flashed through her mind. "Do I have to do their paperwork, too?"

He laughed, a deep rumbling sound that lightened her heart. "No. What they want is advertising. Signs in the yard, notices in the local paper. Permission to publish photographs and give tours through the finished product."

Marilyn leaned against Aunt Phoebe's antique upright

piano. "Max, I don't know." The doorbell rang and three more people entered the house. They all shook hands with Hannibal, thanking him for the opportunity. "All these people," she said. "When will I get any work done?" She clamped a hand to her forehead. "I haven't even arranged the extra time with my office."

"So call."

"My office doesn't open for another hour," she said, glancing into the foyer. The painter, interior designer, and plumber had scattered throughout the house. Now, judging from the pickups and vans outside, a landscape architect, a wood floor refinisher, and a window installer had joined the group. "What do I tell these people in the meantime?"

Before Max could answer, Hannibal poked his head into the music room. "Um, darlin', what's cookin'?"

"What?" She blinked. "Oh, apple turnovers."

Hannibal's eyes lit up. "With cinnamon?"

"Of course," she said. "Coffee's brewing too. Help yourself." Then she remembered his blood pressure. "Wait, aren't you supposed to watch what you eat?"

"You bet. I watch it go right into my mouth."

"Hannibal!"

"What's one turnover going to hurt?"

"Pop, Marilyn's right."

"Come on, Hannibal." She passed him and the myriad of subcontractors, strolled into the kitchen, and opened a small sunflower-decorated canister. "Here, have a cookie. They're low-fat, low-sodium."

"No, thanks," Hannibal said firmly. "I've tried that low-fat stuff. Tastes like sawdust."

"Not these, Pop," Max said as he entered the kitchen. "They're yummy."

"Oh?" She drummed her fingers on the counter. "And just when did you sample them?"

Max looked sheepish. "Well, they were here. I was here."

"There *were* a dozen here," she said. "Now there are two."

He shrugged and spread his arms. "Mice?"

"Good thing they're low-fat," Hannibal said, giving Max a swat on the arm. "Or you'd be splitting your britches."

Marilyn poured herself a cup of coffee.

"No way." Max lifted his T-shirt and thumped his washboard abdomen. "Hard as a rock. Not an ounce of fat on this body."

Marilyn was so shocked, her hand bumped the counter and she dropped her mug onto the floor. It shattered into a hundred pieces, splattering hot coffee everywhere.

"Aaaaahh!" Pain seared her feet and legs. She started to the sink to wet a towel.

"Don't move!" Hannibal said. "You'll cut your bare feet on the broken pieces."

Before she could answer, Max swooped her into his arms and out the back door. "Pop, get the water hose."

She clung to him, her legs burning like fire. Then, suddenly, the fire went out. She blinked. "What happened?"

She stood in the backyard. Max held the garden hose, pointing it at her. She glanced down at clothes. Water dripped off her shorts, and trickled down her legs onto the parched grass beneath her feet.

"That coffee was boiling hot," he said. "You could have blistered."

"Fast thinking, son," Hannibal said from behind her.

"You stay right where you are, darlin'. I'll go clean up the mess."

She gulped. "Thank you."

Max dropped the hose and approached her. She stood rigid, waiting for her heart to start beating again. He'd carried her. He'd protected her, saved her from what could have been a bad burn. No one had ever done anything like that for her.

She didn't know what to think. "Um, Max?"

"Stand still." He crouched in front of her, examining her thighs, shins, and feet. He didn't touch her, for which she was immensely grateful. "You'd better see the doctor."

"It doesn't hurt anymore."

"It might when the water evaporates. And your skin is fire-engine red."

The morning breeze blew hot across her legs. Pain licked up to her thighs. She moaned and crumpled to the ground. "Guess I spoke too soon."

"Come on," he said, scooping her up again. "I'm taking you to the doctor, and no arguments."

"Yes, sir."

When they returned a couple of hours later, Hannibal and the others had left. Though she could walk, slowly, Max carried her in and laid her on the gold damask settee in the parlor. His strength and warmth soothed her, and for several minutes she closed her eyes and allowed herself the luxury of being held.

Then she moved, and fire shot up her legs.

"You have everything you need?" he asked.

She nodded and reached for her cell phone. "While I'm in pain, I might as well call my office."

"I'll be around if you need me."

She smiled at him, then once she was alone she

sighed. No wonder she'd fallen for Max as a teenager. He was a hero. She shook her head and muttered, "Brittany was an idiot."

Dreading it, but knowing she had to do it, Marilyn called her father's office. After a short delay, he answered. "What is it now?"

"I've had a small accident, Father—"

"And?"

"I need more time off."

"No."

"Fine, I'll do my job from here. I brought all the information with me. Whatever else comes up can be faxed to me."

"If you want to keep your job, be back in the office tomorrow."

Frustrated, Marilyn blew out a breath. Is that all he could ever say? "How about a leave of absence until the doctor releases me?"

"Fine. But without pay."

"Without pay, but I'll be working. I've—"

But he'd already hung up.

Just like always, he hadn't listened, didn't even want to take the time to listen. Why did she keep trying? And what would she do for money? Her bank account shrank before her eyes, but her legs burned too much to worry about it. The doctor had bandaged both shins and one thigh. Who knew a few ounces of coffee could do so much damage?

Feeling defeated, she dropped the cell phone and rubbed the bridge of her nose.

The doorbell rang. "Come in!"

"I'll get it." Max charged into the foyer from out of nowhere and opened the door. "Good morning, Mrs. Alford. I'm sorry Pop's not here."

The older woman blushed then clucked her tongue. "I came to see Marilyn." She thumped Max on the chest. "Always knew you were hero material. Story around town says you saved her skin."

"Literally," Marilyn said, trying to sit up.

Mrs. Alford moved next to her and patted her head. "You poor dear, does it hurt?"

Warmth spread through Marilyn. Aunt Phoebe had patted her in just the same way.

"Max Connors, get this girl something, can't you see she's in pain?"

"I'm fine," Marilyn assured her. "The doctor gave me painkillers. And thanks to Max, it's only a first-degree burn—like a bad sunburn."

"Well, you don't worry about a thing, dear," Mrs. Alford said. "I'll help out while you're laid up."

Marilyn blinked, shocked. "Help out? Why?"

"Why? Because we're neighbors." Mrs. Alford pulled the end table closer, handed Marilyn a few magazines, and plumped up her pillow. "You can't cook for yourself while you're in pain."

Marilyn blinked again. Neighbors? She got royal treatment because she was a neighbor? Her neighbors in Chicago never helped her out. A small part of her heart opened up. "Thank you, Mrs. Alford, but please don't go to any trouble."

The older woman clucked her tongue again. "Nonsense. I'm in that house all alone. I can whip up a meal now and then."

She searched the woman's face and understood. Mrs. Alford was lonely. Marilyn knew exactly what that felt like. "No fun cooking for one, is it?"

"I'd rather step on a tack," Mrs. Alford said. "With

both feet." She patted Marilyn's head again. "Now you get some rest and I'll be back about noon."

"Thank you."

After Mrs. Alford left, Marilyn longed to lean back and sleep. The medication had begun to take effect. She felt loose-limbed and drowsy, but she had a very important task to perform.

"Max?" she yelled.

He appeared instantly.

She jumped.

"What's wrong?" he asked.

"How do you do that without smoke and mirrors?"

"Do what?"

"Appear out of nowhere."

He shrugged. "Just trying to be helpful."

"And I'm grateful. Thank you, Max. I could have blistered or worse."

He shoved his hands in his back pockets and looked uncomfortable. "Standard first-aid. I require it of my crew."

"An excellent rule. Mrs. Alford was right. You saved my skin."

He shifted his weight. "You'd have done the same for me."

Would she? She couldn't answer that. She'd relied on herself for so long, hovered on the outside looking in, she wasn't sure she'd act that fast for anyone. "Well, I think I'll stick with iced tea for a while."

"Instant?"

She laughed lightly. "Absolutely. No more boiling water."

"Good, now if you're okay where you are—"

"One more thing," she said, taking a deep breath. "Tell them it's fine with me."

"Tell who what's fine with you?"

She sighed. Her promise to Hannibal, her love for Aunt Phoebe, and Max saving her from a horrible burn added up to one thing. She was destined to restore her aunt's home to its original splendor. So, no matter what deal anyone offered, how much paperwork she had to do, nor how much it cost her financially—or emotionally—she had to go along.

"The people Hannibal brought this morning," she said. "Whatever deal they want to make, I accept."

"Great."

He grinned, leaned down, and kissed her cheek. Her skin tingled, in spite of the numbing of the painkillers.

"Thanks, Marilyn," he said. "You won't be sorry."

"I'm already sorry. This could cost me my job."

He backed off, the light in his eyes dimming. "Your boss didn't like you asking for more time?"

"No, he didn't." She paused, thinking how angry her father had been, how unwilling to listen. Max wouldn't understand that. Which is why she couldn't tell him. She didn't want his pity. Nor did she want to fall for him again, which she could very easily. So, to avoid another broken heart, she had to put distance between them, to thank him and keep him at arm's length.

"Could you do me a favor?" she asked.

"What?"

"Bring me my laptop? I'd like to do some work."

"You're loopy," he said, drawing his ebony eyebrows together. "Marilyn, you're in pain. You should rest, not work. Those pills the doctor gave you are going to kick in and you'll fall asleep at the keyboard."

"I have a job to do," she said, gazing straight into his eyes. "And if I don't do it well, I can't pay you, no matter how big a discount you grant me."

"Right." He stepped back and crossed his arms over his broad chest. "You never let anyone do anything for you, do you?"

"I let you hose me down."

"Did you? Or did I just move too fast for you to object?"

Anger flashed in his eyes, and she realized she'd bungled the explanation. "Max, I didn't mean it that way," she said. "I just want you to understand my priorities."

"I get the picture. You don't want to be 'stuck' here any longer than necessary. Chicago awaits." He crossed the room and halted at the bottom of the stairs. "I won't throw a wrench into the works. I'll give the subcontractors the go-ahead right now. The sooner we get them in here, the sooner you can get back to your career."

"Max, please."

But he'd already left the room. When he returned, he set up her laptop, then used the phone in the kitchen to call the subcontractors. She tried to explain further, but everything she said sounded worse than before. For her comfort—he claimed—he hung plastic over the parlor archways to keep out the dust, then left the house.

Heat swirled within her vinyl prison, and she deserved it for being so tactless. Still, she'd achieved her objective and convinced Max not to waste his time worrying about her. Now he could concentrate on the house, and she'd be safe from his touch, his kisses, and hopefully, his heroic rescues.

She sighed as an ache settled in her chest. If keeping him at a distance was the best for them both, why did it hurt so much for him to shut her out?

A few days later, Max stood outside on a ladder inspecting gingerbread trim. Thunder echoed in the distance, but he barely heard it. His mind focused totally on Marilyn. For the last week, she'd holed up in the parlor or the kitchen. He'd driven her back to the doctor to have her burns looked at, but he got the distinct feeling she would have preferred to go alone.

He sighed and tried to concentrate on the wood in front of him. Why was she so stubborn? He'd seen people shed multiple layers of skin from boiling-water burns. Why did she act like nothing had happened?

The accident played in his mind over and over. She'd screamed, obviously in pain, and her skin had reddened like an overripe tomato. His adrenaline had kicked in and he'd instinctively swooped her into his arms and outside. At that moment nothing else mattered except making sure she was all right. Even after he'd hosed her down and seen how red her skin was, he'd berated himself for moving too slowly, that because of him she'd be scarred for life. Luckily, she wouldn't be, but he could still hear her screams.

Carrying her played over and over in his mind, too. Holding her had been magical, as if they were connected. He'd never felt that way with a woman before. Never.

He thought she'd felt it, too, until they returned from the doctor's office and she'd thrown it back in his face by acting as if nothing had happened. That had hurt almost as much as seeing her in pain.

Confused and a little wounded, he shook his head and climbed down to the ground. "It's rotten," he said to his father. "Gotta replace the whole row. Miller Lumber has some trim the right size, but in pine."

Hannibal nodded. "Won't hold the paint the same as cedar, not to mention weather as well." He made notes on a small pad. "Tried Joe's place over on Commerce Street?"

Max grinned. His father had taken on the task of scrounger. Now he had input on the project, with very little stress, and the perfect excuse to chew the fat with his construction cronies. "Why don't you call them?"

"I will, but first let's check the carriage house. Phoebe tended to collect stuff. Maybe we can find some cedar in there and save Marilyn some money."

"Yeah, okay."

They strolled to the tall, one-story wood-and-brick building, and searched the small storage area in the loft. "Great Scott!" Hannibal exclaimed. "Look at this."

Max's eyes went wide. "The original back door?" He gazed in awe at the thick, six-paneled slab of walnut. Cobwebs and dust covered the back side, and the area around the knob looked a little warped, but the window—stained-glass oval, thick and heavy—made the door nearly priceless.

"It ain't the back door, it's the front," Hannibal said. "By jingo, when they added the powder room off the kitchen, they moved that single panel with the leaded glass to the front and tossed this aside."

"That's criminal."

Hannibal put on a pair of leather gloves and ran his hands down the panels. "Ah, here's the reason."

A small channel, nearly invisible, ran along the inside frame. "Termites?" Max asked. "In that hard wood? They must have been hungry."

"It's damage, all right. We better find out how long this has been up here."

Max groaned. Termites, the terror of Texas. "But if this was the front door, why didn't I find any damage when the crew replaced the porch posts?"

"Could be interior. Could be the fascia board or the

soffit over the frame got wet. You know termites track to water."

"Yeah." If they'd gone untreated all this time, the damage could be extensive. The framing, the interior studs, could be riddled with them. And he'd promised Marilyn no surprises inside the walls. "Guess we'd better call the Bug Man."

"Think they'll want a piece of the action, too?" Hannibal grinned and pointed to the front yard.

Signs dotted Marilyn's lawn like dandelions. Everyone involved with the restoration had stuck their calling card in the ground, each more colorful than the one before.

Hannibal laughed. "Looks like a voting station during elections."

"Pop, this isn't funny. Marilyn's liable to lose her job as it is. If we have to tear out any floors or walls, we'll fall behind schedule."

"That's a shame. She's a good worker."

"Yes, she is." Though she'd barely spoken to him, she'd managed to handle her job, his paperwork, and the dozens of questions involved in renovations.

"She'd make a good bookkeeper," Hannibal added.

Max groaned. "Don't start that again."

"You bet you boots I'm gonna start. You been making goo-goo eyes at her since she nearly burned her legs off."

"It was a first-degree burn, Pop. Don't exaggerate."

"Only because you saved her. Whipped her out to the backyard so fast, it made my head spin."

Max shoved his hands in his back pockets, still awkward at how fast he'd reacted. "Standard first-aid," he said, repeating the words he'd said to Marilyn.

"There's nothing standard about Marilyn."

Max stiffened. He was beginning to find that out. A light wind stirred the trees and he took a deep breath.

"Rain in the forecast?" he asked, hoping to change the subject.

"Maybe," Hannibal said. "The bigger storm's brewing between you and Marilyn. Except you're too stubborn to realize it."

"You're barking up the wrong tree, Pop." Max turned and started for the front of the house and the Connors and Son pickup. Hopefully, his father would climb in and drive away, halting this ridiculous conversation. He and Marilyn had baggage between them, nothing more, just simple remnants of a teenage crush that hadn't quite died out.

"Not to my way of thinking," Hannibal said, walking alongside Max. "I've seen the way she looks at you."

"I don't look at her—" Max stopped. Had he heard right? "The way *she* looks at *me?*"

"Like that summer she tagged after you. Her eyes get so big I worry they're going to jump right out of her head."

Max started walking again. "You're wrong."

"I'm right. I was right then. I'm right now."

"Right?" Max reached the pickup and jerked open the door. "Right about what?"

"You were sweet on her."

"What?" Max shook his head. "*She* had the crush on *me*—a simple teenage crush."

"The teenager grew up, Max."

Memories of Marilyn's rose scent and honey kisses swamped his senses. He cleared his throat. "I noticed."

"About time." Hannibal climbed behind the wheel of the pickup. "So, you going to tell her or shall I?"

Max arched an eyebrow. "That she looks at me funny, or that I noticed she's not sweet sixteen anymore?"

"It was her eighteenth birthday, not sixteenth."

Again, memories swamped him. This time, embarrassment at his own behavior followed. "I remember."

"What happened between you two? One minute Marilyn's happy as a lark, the next she claims a headache and goes to bed."

"The crush ended," Max said. "That's all."

"Bull."

"Go on, Pop, I gotta talk to her and get this sorted out."

"That she looks at you funny or her eighteenth birthday?"

Max rolled his eyes. "The termites. Now, go check on that cedar." He backed up then added, "And drive carefully."

Hannibal saluted smartly. "Yes, sir, boss."

"Oh, stop it."

"You just be nice to Marilyn. She's had a rough time."

Max stopped, crossed his arms, and stared. "Is that the only parental speech you know? You've been spewing it for years."

"And I'll keep spewing it until you start to listen."

Finally, his father drove away, leaving Max standing in the front yard. What would happen next? Because of him, Marilyn worked two jobs, one of which she might lose, and spent her money on a house she never intended to live in. She had people tromping in and out all day long, dust on nearly every surface, nail guns popping, and saws buzzing. And she'd suffered first-degree burns to her legs because he'd made her spill her coffee.

He hadn't quite figured out how he'd accomplished that, but he knew he was at fault.

Moisture-laden wind rocked the metal signs on their stakes. He scanned the cloud-filled horizon, then strolled into the house and scouted out Marilyn's whereabouts.

He checked her plastic-shielded parlor. Wallpaper books, paint samples, and stacks of paper littered the tables, but she wasn't among them. He took a deep breath. The aroma of ginger filled the house. "This isn't fair," he muttered. "Using my stomach against me."

He found her in the kitchen pulling a sheet of gingersnaps from the oven. A checked apron covered her shirt and shorts, and flour dotted her nose and cheek. He sucked air. She looked right at home. Like she belonged.

"Marilyn, it's a hundred degrees outside," he snapped, afraid to think about her belonging in Texas. "Why are you in here in this ... this ... blast furnace?"

"Hello, Max," she said, not reacting to his anger. In fact, she smiled. Why was she so happy? "Come to snitch cookies?"

"I need to talk to you."

"About what?"

She faced him. Her cheeks were rosy pink and her eyes bright. His mind blanked. "About what?" he echoed.

"I don't know, Max. You tell me."

"I ..." He glanced out the window. "Looks like rain."

"Oh, great." She slammed the tray on the counter, and drew off her yellow-checked oven mitts. "A storm, right?"

"Maybe. It's far off yet."

"I hate Texas. Raging heat, dry as a bone, and air conditioners that don't work." To mock her, the unit kicked on. "Then just about the time the day begins to cool off, thunderstorms wreak havoc."

Her vehemence angered him. He couldn't help the weather. "Look, Pop and I were in the carriage house."

"Thought that was a low priority."

"It is, but we were scrounging for—" Lightning split

the late-afternoon sky. The wind whistled around the screen door, and rain pelted the side of the house. He glanced out the window. "Storm came up fast."

She turned to him and grabbed his upper arms. "It's bad news, isn't it? Tell me."

"Well, we found this old door."

"And?" She almost shook him. Thunder banged, moving closer and closer. "And what?" she demanded. "You discovered a cache of stolen goods? Or do I have bats in my belfry?" Heavy storm clouds blackened the sky. She switched on the light. "What is it, Max? Am I going to be stuck here forever?"

Thunder exploded like fireworks, rattling the windows. Rain pounded the cedar-shake roof like a drum. Max yelled to be heard over the noise, but Marilyn obviously didn't hear. Her eyes got wider and wider until, like Hannibal said, they looked like they'd jump right off her face.

Then the lights went out. Mother Nature whipped up the earth outside, but in the house nothing moved, buzzed, or hummed.

"So much for electricity," she said, her voice echoing in the darkened, too-quiet kitchen. "Is that what you wanted to tell me, my wiring's shot? That we'll have to rip open the walls?"

Heat and guilt settled around him. Without air moving, the kitchen felt like a desert, dry, hot and uninhabitable. "Worse."

"Worse?" Her fingernails bit into his arms. "Worse, how?"

He groaned inwardly and prayed he was wrong, because she'd agreed to the restoration on his word that the old house was as solid as a rock.

He took a deep breath and said, "Termites."

Chapter Six

"Termites?" Marilyn's skin crawled and she shuddered. "Little bugs inside my house? Max, you promised me."

"Okay, okay. I admit I made a mistake," he said, frowning. "Do you have to claw me to death?"

"What?" He indicated her hands gripping his forearms. She released him and stepped back. "Max, I'm sorry."

He rubbed the spot. "It's okay."

She stared at the fingernail marks on his bronzed skin, and saw the beginnings of a bruise. "No, it isn't. Max, I've hurt you." She shook her head. "I can't believe it. I've never acted like this."

"Termites have that effect on people," he said lightly.

"No, it's that, and—"

"The house. The constant noise. Being stuck here with me."

"I'm sorry I said that. I've always loved coming here." She caught her breath. "But the storms... on top of everything else."

"Just hang on a few more minutes," he said. "It moved in fast; it'll leave the same way."

She turned to the window. Chills ran up her spine as black clouds blocked out the sun. "It doesn't matter how fast it moves, bad news always follows. All my life, every storm brought a disaster, another event to turn my world inside out."

"It storms here all the time. That's a lot of bad news."

She swallowed, started to speak, then hesitated. Could she trust him with the truth? Yes, he'd been there, he'd understand.

"My mother died during a storm," she whispered. "Chicago doesn't get quite the intensity you do here, but that night sounded like the Fourth of July. I was barely thirteen." A tear slipped down her cheek. "The lightning made her look garish, unreal. As long as I live, I'll never forget her ashen face."

"And I come along and add to your misery with more bad news." He came up behind her and rested his hands on her shoulders. "Marilyn, I'm sorry."

"Thank you, but I'm the one who should apologize." She blew out a breath. "I've been a real grump. Forgive me, Max. I'm not usually like that."

"Forget it." He wrapped his arms around her waist and pulled her closer. "You've been through a lot. It's natural to be on edge." He chuckled lightly. "Though I have to admit, your intensity surprised me. I didn't know you had it in you."

"Neither did I." Heat flushed her cheeks as she remembered how she'd grabbed Max and dug in her nails. "Is there any way I can convince you to forget it?"

"Hmmm, what did you have in mind?"

His voice rumbled against her back, sending tingles down to her toes. This was what she loved about Max.

Loved? No, no, no! She didn't love him.

She cleared her throat and hopefully her mind. "Cookies?"

"Some of these gingersnaps?" he asked. He released her and leaned toward the cookie sheet.

"They say the way to a man's heart—" She bit her tongue. "That's not what I meant."

He obviously didn't catch it, because he didn't respond. Instead, he shoved a handful of gingersnaps into his mouth, and flipped through some recipe cards lying on the counter. "Find some more of Phoebe's prizewinners?"

"Baking relaxes me," she said, hugging herself. The storm blew on through and the lights came back on—as if to reinforce her words. "Mrs. Alford and I are trading recipes, too."

"You know," he said, brushing crumbs from his hands, "you ought to sell some of these."

"I have a job."

"And you're good at it. My paperwork's never been so efficiently and professionally done, but you've got a talent here. These treats are beyond good—they're perfect."

"That's the second time you've mentioned me going into the food business," she said, wondering why he'd make such a strange suggestion. Baking was her hobby, not her profession. "At Sondra's you said I should open a restaurant. What's with you and food?"

"Okay, you caught me. Truth is, I love to eat, but hate to cook, so I'm partial to anyone who feeds me." Reaching for another cookie, he winked. "But I'm not the only one who thinks so. Pop thinks your stuff is out of this world. And the crew—"

"Oh, please. Hungry workers taking a break from the heat don't count."

"Sure they do. You realize Roving Ronny doesn't stop here anymore?"

"That's right." Until he mentioned it, Marilyn hadn't realized it, but she hadn't seen the Ronny's Roving Caterers snack truck for several days. "Are you saying that's because of me?"

"Yep. My guys say compared to your cooking, Ronny's stuff taste like dust and they get enough of that from the Texas wind."

"Really?" She smiled, touched by the compliment. Spending time in the kitchen did make her happy. Not only did it remind her of happy times with Aunt Phoebe, but she enjoyed working with dough, mixing different ingredients, trying new flavorings. "Maybe I'll think about it."

"At least enter something in the bake-off on Fourth of July. You're sure to win—hands down."

"They still do that, huh?" Aunt Phoebe had won first place many times—twice with Marilyn's help. "Does Mrs. Alford still enter her orange-pineapple upside-down cake?"

"Every year. 'Course, your aunt usually beat her out."

"Ah-hah! So that's why Mrs. Alford's been trading recipes with me."

"You gonna let her get away with that?" He grinned. "Your aunt's honor is at stake."

"I said I'll think about it.

"Good, now about the termites?"

Marilyn groaned. "Oh, yes. How much will that cost?"

"I'll call the Bug Man, make sure there's no live critters in the walls, then check for damage."

"The cost, Max?" For a moment, she'd felt a connection with him, as if they were friends and he was giving her advice. But now the house, as always, loomed between them. "Even if he gives me a deal like the others, I'm not sure I can afford it."

"This is one thing you have to do. State of Texas requires a termite inspection before you can sell. Treatment, too, if there are any live ones in the walls."

"And the wood damage?"

"That's my domain," he said firmly. "Any repairs fall under our original agreement."

So, it came down to time—always more time—away from her job, away from starting her own agency, and closer to Max. "Call him. No point in waiting."

"Okay, I've got to check the progress at the other site. The Ferguson house gets windows today. See you tomorrow?"

She nodded and blew out a long breath. "I'm not going anywhere." *Not for a long time.*

Luckily, all the termites were long dead, so Marilyn didn't have to worry about costly treatment. And, according to Max, only the frame around the front door showed any damage. He moved his tools into the foyer and repaired it in an afternoon. She tried not to watch, but she had a clear view from the parlor.

"Think I'll go over Aunt Phoebe's recipes," she said finally. The kitchen would provide a screen from Max's graceful, mesmerizing movements. She only hoped it would screen her thoughts, her fears that she was falling for him again.

"Wait," he said before she could leave the room. "Pop brought this for you." He pulled the form from his back pocket and handed it to her. "Sorry, it's a little crumpled."

And warm from Max's body. She chewed her lip.

"Something wrong?" he asked.

Only that I think I love you. "No. Just wondering what I should enter."

"Try a few." He grinned broadly. "When they heard about the bake-off, the crew selflessly volunteered to be tasters."

She returned his grin. "That's all I need, a group of dusty, stinky men cluttering up my kitchen."

"Exactly what I told them," he said. "*I'm* the boss. I'll do the tasting."

"And split your britches?"

The instant the words left her mouth, Marilyn blushed from embarrassment. "Not that you're in danger of that. I mean, you've . . . you're . . ."

Oh, my. She was babbling again.

"Hey, don't stop now, Marilyn. You're doing wonders for my ego. I haven't been stammered over like that for years."

"No one *ever* stammered over you," she said, disbelief overcoming her embarrassment. "You thought they did, the way you strutted around the construction site."

"And you never hung out there with your friends?"

"I was fourteen. Sondra dragged me there to check out the 'construction hunks.' "

"*Hunk*," he said, puffing out his chest. "Singular. I was the only one."

She rolled her eyes. "Your ego is beyond belief."

"It was then," he said, laughing at himself. "Pop lectured me about preening like some movie star."

"You mean like a Greek god," Marilyn blurted, then slapped her hand over her mouth. How did that get out?

"Excuse me?" Max said, arrogantly arching an eyebrow. "Did you say *Greek god?*"

When would she learn to keep her mouth shut? "Well, that's what some of the girls called you. We'd all been studying mythology in school and the instant I, uh, we saw you, we gained a whole new appreciation for ancient Greece."

"I like it," he said with a smirk.

An urge to tease him overcame her and she bit her cheek to keep a straight face. "Ah, but that was then, Max. Fifteen years can do a lot of damage."

He dropped his hammer, barely missing his foot. "What?"

"Sorry, Max, but the years haven't been kind," she said. "You wouldn't want me to lie."

His face fell and she couldn't help herself, she laughed out loud. "Oh, if you could only see your face."

"Very funny."

"Honestly, Max."

"Yeah, yeah. Don't you have something to do elsewhere?"

"Hmmm, maybe I'll make some humble pie," she said. "Then, as official taster, you can sample it for me."

"Think I'll pass. We Greek gods have to watch our figures."

Oh, please, let me.

She laughed lightly, nervously. "Um, I think I'd better get started on my award-winning entry. See you later, Max."

Fortunately, she escaped to the kitchen before she

blushed bright red. What business did she have teasing Max? She grinned. It had been fun, though, and it felt good, like when Sondra teased her. She sighed. She was falling more and more every minute.

Thank goodness for the bakery idea.

It swirled around in her head, and for the next few days, Marilyn baked cookies, cakes, pastries, and other assorted goodies. Max sampled them. The crew sampled them. Hannibal and Mrs. Alford sampled them, too. Everyone who walked through the door got a taste, and not one person had a bad thing to say.

So Marilyn would enter the contest, but with what? She sat on the kitchen chair and studied her aunt's recipe cards. Which one would best represent "the family honor"?

Max appeared in the doorway. "Madame Baker? Adonis here, ready for my humble pie."

She frowned. "What?"

"I owe you an apology," he said, his face serious.

"Why?"

"When we began this job, I accused you of not caring, of worrying only about yourself."

"What changed your mind?"

"This house."

The house again. Why did everything come back to this renovation? Her revelation of her mother's death, and the Greek god bit, had eased some of her tension around Max. She thought he'd begun to see her as a friend, too.

"I don't understand," she said. "The house hasn't changed."

"Your attitude has." He stepped closer. "Marilyn, I've worked with a lot of people in my life. They all begin to complain about the constant noise, the break in their routine, and the cost. You haven't said a word."

"No, I just clawed you when you told me about the termites."

"That was the storm talking. That doesn't count."

"You're very forgiving."

"And you love this house, don't you?"

She stood, and turned to look out the window. The climbing roses bloomed red and yellow, cheering her. "It's the key to my future, Max."

"Mine, too, but that's not what I mean."

Her future. His future. Understanding swamped her brain. They had a common goal. Instead of fighting him in the beginning, she should have helped, worked with Max to move the project along. Had she delayed her own progress because she refused to see past her old teenage crush?

"I do love this house, Max," she said, turning to face him. "Not just because it's a beautiful piece of architecture, or a representation of marvelous craftsmanship—"

"But because you loved your aunt." He paused. "She was more than just another relative."

"Did Sondra tell you that?"

"No. You did. The way you caress her things, the way you pay attention to the smallest detail in recreating her recipes."

Marilyn sighed. "I used to wish she was my mother, and Sondra was my sister."

"And you lived in Texas year-round?"

"Oh, yes," she said, longing to admit the truth. "I erected an entire fantasy around my summer visits. I'd go to college, get married, and raise a family with—" Realizing who she'd wanted to marry and raise a family with—Max—she halted. "But that was a dream."

"Pop said he tried to convince you to move here."

"He's more of a dreamer than I am," she said, smiling.

"If you like it here, why leave?"

Her smiled drooped. "Because I've outgrown fantasies, Max. I live in the real world. I know Chicago. I'm used to Chicago." And she could blend into the crowd there, be alone among many other lonely people. Not here in Connorsville. Here, her lack of connections, of family, and the ability to create a family stuck out like a sore thumb.

"I see," he said, rubbing a hand over his jaw. "Well, the bottom line is you can take your time paying my bill. Once you get back home, and are settled, we'll work something out."

"No, Max. No favors."

"Marilyn, I've already received three offers to do other restorations. I'm not doing you a favor, I'm repaying you for doing me one."

"What? You think you're in my debt?"

"Without a doubt. Doing this house has given Connors and Son just the boost it needed, so I owe you. Therefore, if I can do anything to make this restoration easier, I will."

Giddy, heady relief spread through her. For the first time since Aunt Phoebe's funeral, she wasn't obligated to anyone.

"I tell you what you can do." She sat quickly, to compensate for her weak knees. "Be a friend and help me decide which one of these to enter."

He grinned and stepped forward to take the recipe cards she handed him. "My skills as a taster are coming into play, huh?"

"I'm stuck," she admitted. "I can't let Aunt Phoebe down. Family honor, like you said. You're familiar with the caliber of entries. Which of these has the best chance?"

He chose a chair across from her and sorted through the cards. After a few minutes, he laid four in front of her. "These."

"Four? I only wanted to enter one."

"One cake, one pie, one cookie, one pastry."

She shook her head. "I can't do that, it's too ostentatious."

"Marilyn, you're a great baker. It would be a crime not to enter every category."

His praise touched her. "You really think so?"

"I swear on my master carpenter's license."

"In that case, I'd better get busy," she said.

"And I'll sharpen my taste buds."

She laughed. "You take your job as taster very seriously, don't you?"

"I take everything seriously," he said, his voice deep and rumbling. "My job, my family." He laid a hand over hers. "And my friends."

Happiness tingled through her, and Marilyn let it. She and Max were friends now, on the same side. It was an unfamiliar sensation, but a good one.

He kissed her cheek. "Gotta go build the booths for the bake-off. See ya tomorrow."

" 'Bye," she whispered.

Happiness warmed her, but would it last? Her summers here had always been an adventure, but autumn and reality had always returned with a thud. Was that why she kept extending her stay? To extend her happy adventure?

Or was she making the biggest mistake of her life by falling for Max, and hoping that, this time, he'd fall for her, too?

* * *

The Fourth of July dawned hot but sunny. Max finished setting up barriers for the parade then hurried to the high school cafeteria for the judging of the bake-off.

Hannibal crossed the crowded room and frowned. "I disqualified myself as a judge."

"Why?"

"Betty Alford entered every category Marilyn did. I can't choose between them. Wouldn't want to try."

Max nodded. He'd judged in years past, but he'd been sampling Marilyn's best efforts all week. He couldn't be impartial. What's more, he didn't want to be impartial. "Yeah, I begged off, too."

Pop arched an eyebrow. "That right? You got some personal stake in the outcome?"

Instead of answering, Max glanced at the judging booths near the kitchen. Marilyn wore a sundress that swirled around her long legs. Red, white, and blue decorated the skirt and the ribbon in her hair. She paced back and forth, wringing her hands.

Hannibal followed Max's gaze. "Poor darlin' is really worked up."

"That's my fault. I told her family honor demanded she enter every category. Didn't know she'd take it to heart."

"She's loyal. Phoebe would be proud."

"Yeah. I'll go tell her that."

"Do. I'll wait with Betty."

Max nodded, and shoved through the contestants and onlookers. "Nervous?" he asked when he reached Marilyn's side.

"Oh, Max, I'm sure I put too much cinnamon in the cinnamon rolls. Those cookies—I used real butter—they'll taste oily. My pie crust is too dry. I—"

He smiled. "Marilyn, calm down. You'll be great."

"And whose idea was it to bake a patriotic-themed cake? A flag made out of strawberries and blueberries on a carrot cake? That's absurd." She ran a hand through her hair, dislodging the ribbon at her nape. "Why did I think I could do this?"

Max picked up the ribbon. "Because you're good. Aunt Phoebe taught you well, and I'm sure she'd be proud of you."

She stopped, her eyes wide. Max's heart lurched. The little-lost-puppy look consumed her face. She obviously feared embarrassing her aunt's memory.

"Do you really think so?" she breathed.

"You bet. Just entering when you have to deal with construction noise, dust, and herds of workers tramping through your house is a triumph," he said. "So . . . wait, the judging's about to start."

Three men and two women inched down the tables laden with baked goods. They each took a taste, chewed carefully, then marked something on a clipboard. Max put his arm around Marilyn's shoulders and felt her stiffen.

"What's taking them so long?" she whispered.

Two judges tasted and retasted Mrs. Alford's entries and Marilyn's—in each category. Marilyn's body felt like a chunk of concrete. "Breathe, Marilyn," Max whispered. "Breathe, honey, or you'll pass out."

He glanced next to him and noticed Mrs. Alford stood stiffly, too. He also noticed Pop had his arm around the older woman's shoulders. Max shook his head.

"May we have your attention," the head judge said from the microphone on the stage. "We apologize for the delay, but two of our contestants showed such creativity and skill, we had a difficult time choosing a winner."

"This is it," Marilyn whispered.

Max held her close.

"We have a tie for first place in each category," the judge continued. "But what pleases me and the other judges most is that the winning tradition has been carried to the next generation. Would Phoebe Howard's niece, Marilyn, and Betty Alford please come forward."

"I won?" Marilyn gazed up at him tears in her eyes. "I tied with Mrs. Alford?"

"You're the best," Max said. "Now collect your prize."

She hurried to the judging stand, a bright smile splitting her face. Mrs. Alford hugged her, and the two women posed with their blue ribbons for the local newspaper. Max took a deep breath and smiled, too. He'd had a hand in it, hadn't he? Though he'd joked about being the official taster, he felt good about encouraging her.

Many of the locals came by to congratulate Marilyn, keeping Max from reaching her side. Finally, the crowd subsided and she held out her hand to him. He took it, and an emotion he couldn't identify warmed him. He told himself it was pride at her win, excitement at seeing her so happy.

Then she reached up and kissed him. In front of the whole town, she flung her arms around his neck and planted a big smack on his lips. He froze in surprise, but a portion of his heart opened wide, too wide. Hurt and pain could slip in at any moment. He tried to push her away, but her words halted him.

"I couldn't have done it without my official taster," she whispered. "Thank you, Max."

Chapter Seven

The crowd hooted and applauded. "No wonder Max disqualified himself as a judge," someone yelled. "He's not impartial."

Max felt his face redden. He gently disengaged Marilyn's arms and stepped back. "Glad to help," he said.

"Oh, Max, I'm sorry. I got carried away." She paused. "You know, the excitement of the moment."

"Guess we're even now."

Her face fell. "Wait. That's not what I meant."

"Yeah?" he said, crossing his arms over his chest. "What did you mean?"

Sondra, Pete, and the kids crowded around to add their congratulations, so Max didn't have a chance to hear her answer.

In fact, for the next three days, he didn't have a chance to be alone with her. He wanted to talk, understand what she meant, but the restoration work took all his time. Plus, the locals stopped in to add more congratulations and borrow recipes. The judges put signs in front of the house—Mrs. Alford's too—proclaiming their bake-off wins. So even when he had the time to get her alone, he didn't have the opportunity.

Replacing the gingerbread trim his father had scrounged up didn't keep him occupied, either. Instead, his mind focused on Marilyn's sweet taste, the warmth of her lips. Had she kissed him, then repeated his horrible apology to get revenge for him rejecting her so long ago? No, he couldn't believe that of Marilyn. She wasn't the vengeful type. Still, he didn't understand how a kiss could turn him inside-out and not affect her, too. "Excitement of the moment" left him feeling cheated.

"Max?"

Marilyn stood on the ground next to the ladder. She shaded her eyes and gazed up at him. "Can you come down?" she asked. "I need to discuss something with you."

"Sure." He climbed down and faced her. Flour dusted her hair and a streak of pink icing marked her chin. He clenched his fist to keep from reaching up and wiping it off. "Bake-off's over, why are you still slaving over a hot stove?"

"Oven," she corrected. "Mrs. Alford and I decided to pool our culinary efforts for next year."

He arched an eyebrow. "But you won't be here."

"She's agreed to carry on the tradition in Aunt Phoebe's name. And Grandma's Treats—you know that little café on Main Street—was very interested in our winning entries. But that's not what I want to talk to you about."

He frowned. Why did her leaving bother him? They'd

agreed the house was their future. She helped him. He helped her, then they would part ways. Friends from a distance. "What's up?"

"Two things." She started walking, and he fell into step with her. "I need the name of a real estate agent," she said. "I thought I'd get appraisals and an idea of asking price, but I'm not savvy enough to know what's reasonable in the local market. Can you recommend someone?"

"Kathleen Griffith at Griffith Realty. She's a real pro."

They'd reached the porch, shading them from the hot July sun. The painters had stripped off the old paint, making the wood look dry and old in comparison to the bright yellow of the siding. A unexplained sadness clouded his mind.

"Those antiques in the attic," she continued. "I like your idea of moving them downstairs."

"I'll get some of the guys on it right away."

"Thank you, but shouldn't I clean them up first?"

He wanted to touch her, to hold her, and he didn't understand why. She wasn't crying, or in need of comfort like before. What was the matter with him?

"Yeah, but that work should be done outside in good ventilation," he said. "Talk to the Connorsville Historical Society. They have people who know all about the proper way to restore antiques."

"Thank you, Max." She paused a minute, gazed at his face, then chewed her lip. "You want some iced tea or something?"

"Maybe some of whatever has the pink icing?"

She rubbed at her chin, then laughed. "I'm an efficient cook, but a messy baker."

They walked inside, but got no further than the front door. The phone rang and Marilyn hurried to the parlor to answer it. Her usual stack of papers cluttered the coffee table, and her computer was on. He paused to watch her, then moved into the kitchen and pulled a pitcher of iced tea from the refrigerator. After her accident with the coffee, and because of the heat, she kept at least one pitcher cold at all times. He glanced out on the back porch and noticed a huge glass jar. Yep, she was making sun tea, a gallon at a time. With the baked goods and the fresh-brewed tea, his crew was going to hate to leave this job.

"Guess what!" Marilyn rushed into the room, her face glowing with excitement.

"What?"

"They did it. You remember the argument I had about the single parent and the insurance problems?"

"Yeah. The benefit package stunk."

"Well, they beefed it up. Gave her the salary she needed and the medical covered she worried about."

"Great."

She clamped her hands on her hips. "Max, don't you see? They took my advice. They put aside their stupid statistics and looked at the person they were hiring. I made a difference."

A difference? Is that what she wanted to do? Is that why she was gung-ho to start her own company, so she could make a difference in the world? He glanced over at the platter of iced sugar cookies. He supposed baking good food and winning contests couldn't compare with helping people find jobs.

Again, sadness clouded his mind.

"That's great," he said, swallowing his disappointment. He was an idiot to think she'd stick around Texas just to bake cookies. "Good for you."

"It's marvelous. Someone listened to me for a

change." She laughed lightly. "I suppose that sounds silly to you. You've run your crew for years. Everyone listens to you."

"No, it doesn't sound silly." But it bothered him. Why was she so hot to go back to a job where they didn't pay attention to her suggestions? "Guess that's why you want to start you own recruiting agency."

"That's a big part of it." She moved past him and indicated the cookies. "Here, try one of these. A new low-fat, low-sugar recipe Mrs. Alford gave me. Apparently she thinks Hannibal could lose a few pounds."

"No thanks."

"Please?" She held up a hammer-shaped cookie. "I know pink looks silly on a hammer, but I ran out of food coloring. Please? I'd really like your opinion."

"No, thanks. I need to get back to the trim so the painters can finish up that side." He moved to the back door. "Oh, and I'll have a couple of guys move whatever you want from the attic to the back porch. You can work there without worrying about fumes, and still protect the furniture from the weather."

"All right," she said slowly. "Max, have I done something wrong? Are you angry with me?"

He swallowed hard and tried not to look at her. The truth was, he didn't want her to leave, but asking her to stay just to bake cookies for him to nibble on sounded absurd. In any case, she couldn't afford to do anything unless she sold this house.

"I'm tired," he said, using an old excuse. "This is my busy time of year."

"Of course," she said. "I shouldn't keep you."

He nodded, then walked out with her words echoing in his head. "I shouldn't keep you," she'd said. But he had the oddest feeling that's exactly what he wanted her to do. Keep him. Hold him. Forever. And those feelings scared him to death.

July flew by in a hot blur. Marilyn worked hard on Max's papers, Aunt Phoebe's recipes, and last but not least, on finding jobs for her clients. Placing that single mother had made her feel wonderful, until her father called to okay her extended stay in Texas, stating that apparently she worked better out of the office than in. His words had hurt, and she continued to put in calls, send out letters, and schmooze with the CEOs of big firms looking for new talent, but her heart wasn't in it.

Instead, she rose early each morning still feeling her lips on Max's, and stayed up late each evening imagining him kissing her back. She made iced tea for the crew, whipped up apple turnovers and cookies for break times, and made sure she had a reason to be wherever Max was. She knew she resembled the tag-along she'd been as a teenager, but she couldn't help herself.

When the crew left at night, the house was too calm, too still. She wandered through the half-finished rooms rubbing her arms against the lonely silence. When she started her own agency, she'd rent office space in a mall, or on a noisy corner. Quiet reminded her too much of her lack of connections.

One early August evening, she stepped out onto the back porch. A sideboard, two end tables, and a magnificent dry sink sat under plastic cover. She'd been advised not to touch them beyond a simple cleaning, that the marks and weathering of the wood added to the value and the look. With Hannibal's guidance, Marilyn had dusted and oiled them until she could see her reflection in the rich, dark wood. Now they waited until the floors could be refinished, and the new wallpaper hung. Before long, Kathleen could put the house on the market, and Marilyn would be on her way back to Chicago.

She sat on the top step and took a deep breath. Dry, dust-laden air infiltrated her nose and she sneezed. It hadn't rained in over three weeks. The grass suffered, but the crickets and the cicadas seemed to flourish. She sighed as their singing filled her ears.

"Not executive recruiting tonight?" a voice asked from the darkness in front of her.

"Max?"

"Yeah, it's me," he said. "You got a minute?"

Her heart thumped. Though she'd spent a lot of time in the same room with him, they hadn't been alone since she'd kissed him at the Fourth of July bake-off. His surprised look still flooded her mind, along with his frown when she'd admitted to getting carried away. She couldn't believe those words had leaped from her mouth. How could she have been that mean to him? It had happened to her too many times—once from Max, and the worst from her ex-fiancé, who'd claimed her infertility didn't matter and then explicitly pointed out that particular flaw in his cruel rejection.

If only she could apologize without sounding sorry for kissing him. She wasn't. She would never be sorry for kissing Max, only for letting herself get hurt again.

She stood. "It's a hot night. You want some iced tea?"

"Sure." He stepped onto the porch and settled on the swing in the corner. It creaked as he pushed it back and forth. "You must be out a boatload of bucks making tea for all of us."

"I can't help it. I see you and your crew working in this heat, and I get thirsty. Before I know it, I have two or three gallons made, more than I can possibly drink."

"You're a good person, Marilyn."

"Thank you."

Uncertain what to expect, she lounged near the door. The light from the kitchen window threw a golden shadow on the porch and from it, she could make out the expression on Max's face. He looked grim. Serious. She sniffed the air. No moisture. No storms. The setting wasn't right for bad news.

"What's wrong, Max? You seem upset."

"Worried."

"About?"

"You."

"Me?" Surprised, she blinked. "I'm fine."

"Be honest, Marilyn. Did you lose your job?"

"No. Why would you ask that?"

He sighed and ran a hand over his jaw. "Because you've spent most of your time with me, uh, with the house this month. But when I first started this job, the phone rang constantly. It hardly ever rings now. I was afraid . . ." He paused. "I'd hate it if you got fired because of me."

His concern touched her. "I'm still employed, Max. In addition to that single parent, I placed two more people."

"You have?" The porch swing stopped. "Then why have you had that look?"

"What look?"

"Like you wanted to tell me something."

She blew out a long breath and indicated the space next to him. "May I?"

"Sure."

Oh, bad idea. Since he left her house that afternoon, he'd showered. Now, he smelled clean and fresh and exciting. Her mind swam with the aroma and her throat closed up. How to begin?

"You did get fired," he said flatly. "You're trying not

to make me feel bad, but even in the moonlight, I can see bad news written all over your face."

"I *do* want to talk to you, but not about my job." Placing her glass on a metal side table, she turned to him, bringing her knee up onto the swing's hunter green cushion. "I've been trying to come up with the right way to apologize."

"For what?"

She chewed her lip. "For hurting you at the bake-off."

"You kissed me. It didn't hurt."

"Oh, Max, you know what I mean," she said, uncertain if he was being noble, or if he'd truly been unaffected. "I behaved badly."

"You got carried away," he said stiffly. "It happens."

"But I lied to you."

"You lied? About what?"

"I didn't get carried away, I took advantage of an opportunity. And since then, I've been tagging along, just like that summer when I first saw you, hoping I'd get another chance."

"So you didn't lose your job."

"No!" She forced herself to stay calm. "Max, forget about my job and listen. I kissed you *on purpose,* because I wanted to. I still want to."

Silence cloaked them both. Nothing moved—not the wind, the cicadas, or the crickets. One minute passed and he didn't respond. Two minutes passed. Still silent. Shadows over most of his face prevented her from reading his expression, and she was beginning to regret speaking up.

Her heart thumping loudly, she decided to push the issue. "Max. Did you hear me?"

"I heard," he said, clearing his throat. "And I couldn't

help remembering another time you wanted to kiss me. Your eighteenth birthday."

"Oh, *that*." Marilyn now gave thanks for the darkness, because heat flushed her cheeks, and she knew she was blushing all over. "Please, I behaved like a love-struck child. I—"

"I lied, too."

"What? When? Max, what are you talking about?" He scooted closer to her, and laid an arm on the back of the swing. His fingers brushed her shoulder and she tingled. "Max?"

"That night," he murmured, "you told me you felt like a woman and wanted a grown-up kiss, worthy of your new status."

"Yes." Her blush deepened as the memory of her humiliation raced through her mind. Her lips on his, then the pain of his rejection. "You were twenty-two, a college grad. To me, you represented the worldly expert."

"And I wanted to burst your fairy-tale view of the world."

"Why?"

"I worried about you. You always looked vulnerable, so lost. I was afraid you'd get hurt, that someone would take advantage of you."

"So you decided to show me how cruel the world could be?"

"Not cruel, just real."

"Yeah, well, you proved that," she said, still reeling from the hurt. All that summer Max had let her tag along, let her be part of the group. She'd felt certain he'd understand her wishes. Except he'd shoved her away. "Are you telling me I need another lesson?"

"No, no!" He sighed deeply. "Look, I know I hurt you, but it wasn't intentional. I'd had a rough year. I'd just come home from college where everyone I'd met was going off to exciting cities and adventurous jobs. Instead of going with them I had to come home to Connorsville and Pop's business."

Marilyn gasped, almost too surprised to speak. "*You* didn't want to come home?"

"Not that summer. Until my senior year, all I ever wanted to do was build houses with Pop, but after graduation, after watching my friends take off for new futures, I felt cheated, like I was missing out on something. So, instead of getting right to work, I copped an attitude."

"*You* rebelled?"

"Pop and I fought all summer."

"I don't believe it." She sat back and let her mind roam over that summer, trying to remember Hannibal and Max together, trying to recall a difference in their behavior. "Oh, my goodness," she breathed after a few minutes. "Your hair. That's the summer you let your hair grow."

"Yeah." He chuckled and flipped his ponytail. "Pop threatened to hack it off with a jigsaw, but I didn't give in. That's the only fight I won."

"I had no idea."

"I know you didn't," he said, his voice turning serious again. "But that doesn't excuse the way I acted that night."

"Don't worry about it," she said, eager to get off the subject. How much more could she endure? Being close to Max and confessing her attraction was difficult enough. But to hear that her first, mature, woman-to-man kiss had been a life lesson hurt. A lot. All these years she'd secretly hoped he'd been at least a little impressed with her fervor, if not her skill. "Your solution worked. My eyes were opened, I—"

"It wasn't a solution," he interjected quietly. "Marilyn, don't you understand what I'm trying to tell you? Claiming you were too young was the only excuse I could think of."

"Excuse?"

"Excuse," he whispered, taking her hand. "I was amused by your request, and a little flattered, but I'd expected an inexperienced peck. You knocked me for a loop, Marilyn. You were so sweet, I wanted to kiss you forever. It scared me, so I pushed you away."

Her mind whirled with disbelief. "Max, are you telling me, I mean, are you sitting here admitting that you enjoyed that kiss?"

"Yes," he said, his voice ragged. "And each one since."

"Oh, my." He leaned toward her, his lips so close his warm breath brushed her face. Her heart leapt and jumped, searching for an even rhythm. "I don't know what to say."

"Then don't say anything."

Her breath caught. Could this really be happening? Could Max have cared all along—including now? His lips touched hers and all thoughts ceased. Instead, she allowed herself this one moment, to believe, to believe that she could have her dream. Unfortunately the moment passed all too quickly, and in its place came reality.

"Oh, boy," she murmured.

He raised his head and stroked her cheek. "What's wrong?"

"Oh, Max, I've dreamed of this for years, but . . ." She took a deep breath and edged away from him. Even if he did care, they couldn't be together. Better to stop now before anyone got hurt. "But it won't work."

"Why? Oh wait, I know." Mirth filled his voice and he chuckled. "It's because I'm not a Greek god anymore. Right?"

Marilyn laughed, then sobered. "No, my concern isn't about mythology, but about geography."

"Right." His light tone dropped and he let out a long breath. "You have a job, commitments in Chicago."

"And you belong here. In Connorsville."

"I can't leave and you can't stay."

"We have no future. There's no point in pursuing this."

She wished they *could* pursue it. Just like when she was a teenager, she wanted her idyllic Texas summers to last forever.

"No point," he agreed. "So what do we do now?"

"I know this is usually a brush-off phrase," Marilyn said, drawing in another deep breath, "but can we be friends?"

"Absolutely. And maybe get to know each other again?"

Relieved and warmed by his positive response, Marilyn smiled. "I'd like that."

"Great." He kissed her cheek then stood. "Good night, Marilyn."

"Good night, Max."

He strode down the steps and was quickly swallowed up by the darkness, but Marilyn sat there long after he'd disappeared. Friends. Friends with Max. Incredible. In a perfect world, she'd achieve her dream, belong somewhere, to someone. To Max.

But it wasn't a perfect world, and even if it were, she had one deep-seated fear, one she rarely admitted to herself. What if she simply didn't have what it took to have a loving, lasting relationship? What if she tried to have a future here with Max, and wound up hurting the people she loved most?

That's one risk she *wasn't* willing to take.

So, better to accept her limits and end any romantic involvement here and now. Better to just be friends and cherish the good times. That would be enough. It had to be.

Chapter Eight

Max arrived at Marilyn's earlier than usual the next morning. Clearing the air between them had felt really good, like a fresh start. So he'd arrived before the rest of the crew so they could start off their new friendship.

When she answered the door, though, eyes half open, looking rumpled and cute, he forgot all about friendship and kissed her.

"Max?" she mumbled then pushed him away. "Hey!"

"Sorry." Great, less than twenty-four hours into their "fresh start" and he'd already broken the agreement. "I, uh, haven't had coffee yet."

Lame excuse.

"Nobody's had coffee yet. For goodness sake, the slender pink fingers of dawn haven't even spread over the horizon yet."

He rolled his eyes. "Slender pink fingers?"

"Hey, you wake me up, you take what you get."

"It's not that early."

"It's *five-thirty!*" She tried to open both eyes, but only managed one. "If I make coffee, will you tell me why you're here at five-thirty in the morning?"

"I just wanted to get started on our new friendship?" he offered.

"At five-thirty in the morning?"

"Before the crew came. Hard to have any conversation after that."

Her other eye opened, but the first closed again. "Next time I agree to be friends with someone," she said, yawning, "I'm going to put some time limits on it."

"Good plan," he said, chuckling lightly. "You said something about coffee?"

"Yeah, follow me." Both her eyes finally opened and she padded into the kitchen. "You fix the coffee, and I'll heat up a couple of turnovers."

"Gladly."

After a cup of coffee and two pastries, Marilyn seemed to be able to focus. She opened the back door and took a deep breath. "You know, in spite of my complaints to the contrary"—she flashed him a smile—"early morning has become my favorite time of day. Before you and your crew descended on me I never appreciated how sweet the air smelled, or how refreshing the cool wind felt on my face."

"In college I drove my roommates crazy getting up with the sun," he said from his seat at the kitchen table. "It's natural. I like it."

"I'm so glad we're going to be friends and spend time together."

She moved toward him and he started thinking about

their agreement, and wished she could stay longer. He wanted to share more quiet mornings with her.

"But we won't have much time to spend together, will we?" she added after taking the seat across from him.

"Not if either of us intends to sleep." He realized the implication of his words and hurried to add, "I meant—"

"Oh, you're so cute when you blush."

"I am *not* cute. And men don't blush."

"Especially Greek gods?"

"You said I wasn't one anymore."

"I lied." She grinned. "But I won't argue. I feel too good to argue."

He started to take her hand, then remembered himself. "I feel good, too, but I wanted to make sure last night hadn't upset you, that—"

"That I understood the limits of our relationship?" Her voice flowed like warm molasses, just like his father had said. "We're friends, Max. Friends who, because of differing commitments, have agreed to remain just friends. Why are you concerned?"

"We talked about a lot of things, emotional things, and in the light of day things can look different. Can cause regrets."

"You're right, but I'm glad we cleared the air. Really, I don't regret one thing I said last night."

"Good." He blew out a breath, but the relief he'd expected to feel didn't quite come. Why, he wasn't sure. "So, let's do something together tonight."

She winked. "Wanna meet on the porch swing at midnight?"

"You have the strangest sense of humor," he said, shaking his head. "And it pops up at the oddest times."

"Like I said, it's early—"

"And I have to take what I get, right?" He laughed,

delighted. Where had this particular Marilyn been hiding all this time? "How about we go out and have supper."

"At nine o'clock at night? I'd starve before then."

"We'll go to Sondra's. Have a Wild West supper and throw peanut shells on the floor."

"You want to start gossip?"

He arched an eyebrow. "*Who* kissed *whom* in front of the whole town?"

"Oh, yeah, that *was* me, wasn't it?"

She blushed and he loved it. He loved her.

His heart stopped and he nearly dropped his coffee mug. No! Love hurt, had destroyed him before. Sure, he was attracted to her, definitely enjoyed being with her. That wasn't love.

She tapped her chin with her index finger. "Why do you suppose no one's mentioned that? Sondra didn't even call me. And she loves to tease."

"Pop put out the word to leave you alone," Max said.

"You're making that up. This may be your town, but Hannibal doesn't have that kind of pull."

Max laughed. "True. People probably realized it was a spur-of-the-moment thing. I wouldn't worry about it."

"All right, I won't. So supper tonight on Mount Olympus with the other gods? Shall we have ambrosia and . . ." She waved her hand in the air. "Oh, whatever else you gods eat."

"You're a nut, did you know that?"

"But a charming one, right? That's what you'll tell the newspapers when they drag me away? 'She was so charming I never realized she'd lost her marbles.'"

Max put a hand up to his ear. "Listen, I think they're coming for you now."

She laughed. "Well, let's have breakfast. I'll put the eggs on the sidewalk and let the Texas sun fry them."

"You just said it was a cool morning."

"Relative to the Sahara, yes. But face it, Max. Texas in August is hot, hot, hot."

"Thanks for that tidbit. I've only lived here all my life."

She clucked her tongue. "So young, so handsome, and so totally out of his mind. Poor Max."

He placed a hand on her forehead. "I've never heard of sunstroke hitting so early in the day—and inside an air-conditioned house—but you're showing all the signs."

"So, I act silly when I feel good. Is that a crime?"

"Not even close." Mesmerized by the laughter in her eyes, he stepped closer, wanting to kiss her so badly, he couldn't think of anything else. Luckily, she blinked and he came to his senses. Scolding himself for almost breaking their agreement—again—he backed up. "Well, I'd better get to work or you'll never get back to Chicago."

"Now that," she said with a grin, "would be a crime."

"Yeah." His heart broke a little, and confusion swam in his head. How could he have these feelings when she was all wrong for him, and after they'd agreed to just be friends? Thank goodness he had work to do elsewhere this morning, so he could clear his head, get his priorities straight. "Tonight," he said as he left. "Supper. Don't forget."

"I won't."

And neither would he. He thought about nothing else the rest of the day, especially her remarks about Chicago. He was glad she'd reminded him. She wasn't staying. Their relationship would never be permanent, and he didn't love her. He couldn't. He didn't have enough strength to survive another broken heart.

Supper had to be canceled due to a problem with the Ferguson house—another change—but Max didn't mind too much. When he arrived at Marilyn's later, she'd set up a small table on the back porch. They drank iced tea and nibbled on Mrs. Alford's version of orange-pineapple upside-down cake.

"Hmmm, this is nice," he said, licking his lips.

"Oh, yes, the porch swing is a special place."

"That's right," he said, caught up again in her expressive gray eyes. "That fateful evening was here on the swing."

"Um-hmmm." She scooted closer. "As I recall, it went something like this."

Her lips brushed his and he didn't need any more encouragement. He threaded his hands through her hair, dislodging her usual ribbon, and kissed her with all the affection he had—more than he realized. "You have a great memory," he murmured.

"Hmm? Oh!" She groaned and pushed him away. "Apparently not."

"What?" Max hovered above her lips, waiting to kiss her again. Then it hit him. Their agreement. "We did it again."

"My fault this time. Sorry, Max."

"Well," he said, rising to stand near the porch rail and put a little distance between them. "Now we're even. What do you say we do something else with our lips?"

"Max, Max, Max," she said, tsking, "you've already had three pieces of cake."

He laughed. "I meant, talking, you know, sharing information?" He wanted to know her, to understand why she had to go back to Chicago when she seemed to love Texas so much. "Tell me about your job."

"Boring, I hate it."

"What? Then why go back?"

"Because I have to finish what I started. And then

move on. I've worked for years, Max, to build up a client list that I can take with me when I start my own company. When I say I hate my job, I mean the building, the place, not the work I do."

"So tell me about that."

"I started out to please my father. You understand about that, I'm sure."

"Absolutely."

"You see, my father married my mother because he got her pregnant. He insisted it was the right thing to do, and they'd be fine."

"But?" Max asked, hearing the bitterness in her voice.

"Father resented her, accused her more than once of trapping him. After she died, he turned his resentment on me. I tried to make it up to him, to be as little trouble as I could—"

"But he sent you to Aunt Phoebe."

"Yes." Marilyn stood and began to pace. "I know now she loved me, tried to help me through my mother's death, but I thought it was a token, a role she'd been forced into."

"Why? I mean, I remember her talking about your visits, planning parties for you meet to people. Phoebe may have been reserved, but—"

"Not reserved. Shy and lonely. I felt it then, and I know it now. But Father convinced me she was just a paid baby-sitter."

"So you kept your feelings to yourself."

"I didn't want to believe it about Aunt Phoebe, but disbelieving meant my father lied to me, that he didn't want me. That truth would be too much to bear, so, I accepted his lies and kept on trying."

"Trying? Trying what"

"To get him to love me."

Stunned, Max blinked. How could a father not love his own child? No wonder she'd seemed lost and alone. She'd felt unloved.

"To this day," she added, "he blames Mother and me for ruining his career."

"Ruining his career? How?"

"I don't know. You see, he owns RSW, Inc. *Is* RSW, Inc."

"What? Your father *owns* the conglomerate you work for?"

"Yes, he did well in spite of us. That's why I kept trying to reach him, because it simply didn't make sense for him to continue blaming me." Sighing, she stopped pacing and dropped onto the swing. "Truth is, he was a part of my fantasy, too. I thought I could reach him if we shared a common goal."

Max sat and pulled her close. "I had no idea."

"I never talked about it, and neither did Aunt Phoebe. I think she kept hoping he'd come around."

"That's why you're close to Pop."

"Remember I said I fantasized about a family? Aunt Phoebe was my mother, Sondra my sister, and—"

"Pop was your dad."

"Yes. He treated me so nice, and he knew—all about my father. I didn't realize it until I saw him in the hospital, but somehow he guessed."

"Yeah, that's Pop," he agreed, stroking her hair. "Reads people like a book."

Everything came together for Max. He understood a lot about her drive, her need to set up shop in Chicago, and why he'd thought her to lack family values. Tough to have family values when you don't really have a family. "You going to prove yourself to your father?"

"No. I learned my lesson on that score. Reaching out

to him is like trying to grab thin air." She paused. "I need to prove myself to me. I can do it, Max. I know I can. I care, and I understand how hard it is to work at a place you hate."

"Yeah, you'll be great," he said, having a hard time keeping the disappointment out of his voice. He wanted to love her, the emotion pushed to get out, but she had no reason to stay in Texas, and an opportunity to succeed in Chicago. If he let himself feel that deeply for her, he wouldn't survive the hurt when she left. "Just do me a favor and be careful, okay?"

"I promise." She gave him a quick smile. "But don't forget, I'm a bake-off winner. I withstood one-hundred-degree Texas heat amid construction noise and dust, and managed to bake four winning entries. I can handle anything." She snapped her fingers. "Piece of cake."

Her words held assurance, but her voice didn't. What else could she be holding back? She'd confessed her fear of storms, her problems with her father. Had she had a bad love affair like he had? Had some man touched, then ripped apart, her heart?

"And don't you forget I'm a Greek god with powers of mythic proportions. If you ever need help, you know who to call."

"1-800-Greek-god?"

"Right." He gave her a friendly kiss on her forehead and stood. "Well, if we're going to get you out of here and in business, I'd better go home and get some sleep. Can't get the house into shape if I can't focus."

"Yeah, wouldn't want you to fall asleep on the job and drop a hammer on your foot," she teased. "It wouldn't be very godlike."

He laughed and paused on the porch step. "Hey, tomorrow is Sunday. Come to church with me. We'll sit in the family pew."

"I'd love to, but do you think that's wise? In this town, isn't that like declaring to everyone that we're a couple?"

"You're right," he said, disappointed again. "No point in sending out the wrong message. What do you suggest?"

"What we're doing now. Talking together after you finish your work."

"Okay. If that's the way you want it."

"That's the way it has to be."

"Right."

Max left for home, confused. She was holding something back, something she couldn't or wouldn't tell him. Brittany had behaved the same way, withholding her secret—which was she'd never intended to stay in Connorsville at all.

Well, he already knew Marilyn wasn't staying, so maybe he didn't need to know her secret. Though if he'd known Brittany's he might not have fallen so hard. Yeah, secrets hurt, not helped. So, for his own sake, he resolved to find out Marilyn's, and as soon as possible.

He spent every spare moment with her. From early morning, till well into the night, Max found ways to get next to Marilyn. Before he knew it, August had become September, and still he hadn't discovered her secret. They talked. Every evening, they sat in the swing and traded bits of their lives. Their discussions ranged from favorite foods to favorite books to favorite escapes. Hers was the attic where her aunt had stored all the memorabilia. His was the huge elm, the one his great-grandpa had planted behind his family home.

It was obvious to him—especially when they forgot their agreement and kissed—that they were becoming much more than friends. He wanted to talk about it, to discuss the future, but each time he brought it up, or had it on the tip of his tongue to ask her to stay, she changed the subject.

So, on this September afternoon, he'd decided to face the problem head-on. The restoration was complete, except for a few final touches. He had no excuse for delaying. If he didn't tell her how he felt, she'd leave and make her life in Chicago. When he pulled up to her house, however, he lingered, practicing one more time what he wanted to say. Then he squared his shoulders, strolled up the walk, and opened the front door.

She was in the parlor with the real estate agent.

"Max, you remember Kathleen," she said.

He nodded. "Good to see you again."

"You've done a great job, Max," Kathleen said. "I can't wait to set up an open house."

He moved to greet Marilyn, but she kept her distance. Confused, he looked her over and understood everything. Instead of her usual T-shirt and shorts, she wore a suit, like when she'd arrived. It was her way of saying, "Summertime fantasy's over. Time to get back to Chicago."

"I'm so excited," she said. "Kathleen thinks I'll get my asking price easily. I owe it all to you, Max. Thank you."

"You're welcome," he said stiffly. "Now if you'll excuse me, I'll check on the kitchen."

He walked away, disappointed not to get her alone, and hurt she seemed so anxious to leave. He halted at the kitchen doorway and listened to their conversation.

"The kitchen was the last room to redo," he heard her say. "I put it off as long as I could because I love baking—"

"The bake-off proved that," Kathleen said. "But I thought—" She paused, and Max strained to hear.

"Didn't Grandma's Treats approach you? They raved about your low-fat cookies."

"Oh, that. I think Hannibal put them up to it," Marilyn said, her voice full of disbelief.

Max knit his eyebrows. What was in Marilyn that made her hold back? Why couldn't she believe that people raved about her baking because it was out-of-this-world delicious?

"Besides," he heard her say, "I'm not set up for that kind of commercial baking. It's a hobby, something I do for fun."

Frowning, Max moved farther into the kitchen and ran a hand over the newly painted cabinets. Marilyn had chosen white, in keeping with the tradition of Victorian style. The stove resembled an old wood burner, but cooked with gas with six burners and a double oven, and the refrigerator looked like an old-fashioned icebox. Inside, it held the latest subzero technology. The countertops echoed the black and white floor, and a cook top island—with an overhead pot rack and two specially slotted cabinets for baking pans—dominated the center of the room.

Not set up for commercial baking? A person could bake for an army in this kitchen. Why would Marilyn say it couldn't?

He heard the front door open and close, so went to find her and get the answer to that question, and maybe a couple of more. He found her on the back porch, on her cell phone.

"Yes, the house is finished. Yes, I know you thought it was a waste of time, but it's over now."

Walking as she talked, her pumps thumped on the porch floor, and her voice sounded stiff and stilted. Max leaned against the back door, waiting for her to finish circling the house and wondering who upset her so badly.

He could only hear bits and pieces, so her conversation didn't make sense to him. When she passed by him the second time, he reached out and touched her arm.

"Marilyn?"

"What!" Her eyes went wide and she clutched the front of her suit. "Oh, Max. You startled me."

"Sorry."

"No, I was talking to Max," she said into the phone. With a pleading look, she held up one finger, motioning him to wait. "Max Connors, the contractor for the house. Yes, he knows what he's doing. Fourth-generation construction firm, Father."

Father?

Had she called him or the other way around? Either way, a sense of dread coiled in Max's gut, a sense that no matter what he said now, Marilyn would never consent to stay in Texas.

"What?" she said into the phone, her voice rising. "But you granted me a leave of absence, you can't—What? They're cutting how many jobs? Oh, my. Yes. Yes, I'm through here. Of course I'll be in the office on Monday."

She punched the OFF button and collapsed onto the swing. End of the line. Time to go. Quit. 'Bye. Max stiffened, unable to bring up the subject. Instead, he moved across from her to lean against the porch support. Her rose scent washed over him and his heart broke.

Well, at least this time he hadn't asked a woman to stay and been laughed at.

"Landscaping will have to wait until cooler weather," he said, his voice ragged, "or the plants will die. But the house is done."

"It looks great, Max," she said, her voice cool and professional. "I'm glad I did the entire restoration."

"Yeah."

Tilting his head back, he gave his handiwork a long look. Pale blue covered the ceiling, imitating a clear summer sky. Burgundy, dark green, and a deep tan highlighted the intricately turned posts and railings. The tan continued on the gingerbread siding with the other two colors as accents. The front door had been moved to the back and the stained glass one, now refurbished thanks to his and his father's carpentry skills, hung in the front once again.

"Took longer than I thought," he said after a long pause, "but even if I say so myself, it looks pretty good."

"Aunt Phoebe would be proud."

"Yeah. Sure."

"Max? Something wrong?"

I love you. I want you to stay. I want us to be a couple.

But he couldn't tell her that. She wanted to leave, needed to leave. From what he'd heard of the conversation with her father, she still had issues to settle with him. Max understood the special bond of working in the family business, and if she still thought she could make that connection, well, he couldn't get in the way of that, couldn't even ask her to consider staying in Texas. Nor could he bear to ask and hear her sweet voice tell him no.

Either way, there was absolutely no point in bringing up the subject.

"I have the end-of-the-job blues," he said instead, which was only stretching the truth a little. "This house is finished. The six customs are down to the painting, carpet, and landscaping. It's like opening presents on Christmas. Once the paper's thrown away and everyone's said thank you, the excitement's gone."

"But Connors and Son will expand," she said, her gray eyes widening in concern. "You'll have more contracts than you know what to do with."

"As a matter of fact, I have an appointment with two homeowners next week about restoration. And Pop's got a lead on five lots that another builder had to let go. We might be able to take them over and build right through the winter."

"As I suspected. You'll be busier than ever."

"Yeah, sure." But it would be just a job—cold and impersonal—without Marilyn's sweet smile to begin and end his day. He sighed and started to sit on the porch swing, then thought better of it. "Set up everything with Kathleen?"

"Open house Sunday. Think I can get a cleaning crew in here before then?"

"This house will sell within minutes of you putting it on the market—dirty or clean."

"Then there's nothing left for me to do but—"

"Leave."

"Yes. I'm taking the first flight out tomorrow morning." She laid a hand on his arm, and it took all his control not to pull her into his arms and kiss her senseless. "It's what we agreed."

"Yes. Yes, it is," he said, holding out his hand. "Goodbye, Marilyn. Best of luck in your new business."

"Good-bye, Max," she answered, and leaned up to kiss his cheek. "Thanks. For everything."

"No problem."

As though he lost the woman he loved every day of his life, he smiled, released her and walked away. But instead of heading to the construction site, he escaped to his favorite spot—Great-Grandpa's elm. He desperately needed to be alone, to figure out how he'd put his heart back together after Marilyn left.

Chapter Nine

Marilyn watched Max go, feeling as though she'd walked in at the middle of a movie. Somewhere she'd missed some piece of dialogue, some important bit of background information. But what? She and Max had agreed they had no future, that they would just be friends. That's what they'd done.

So why did she feel as though something had gone wrong, as though she'd broken a promise?

Admittedly, the phone call from her father hadn't helped her mood any. She'd thought herself free of those ties, of wanting to try with him again.

Confused, she shook her head and took a long walk around Aunt Phoebe's house. From the stained-glass front door, to the refurbished kitchen, to the freshly painted back porch, the Victorian shouted life, love, and happiness. Upstairs, she rubbed her hands along the varnished railing and the floral wallpaper, etching their textures in her mind.

Her last stop, the attic, nearly broke her heart.

Devoid of furniture, memorabilia, and cobwebs, it looked lost and lonely. Her heels clicked on the polished wood, and echoed in the emptiness. She raised the window and leaned out to gaze at the neighborhood beyond. Who would fill this room with memories now? A young executive bent on turning quick profit? A historian or architect who loved the era?

No, a family. A mother, a father, and children must occupy this home and fill it with the love she'd never known. Resolved, she walked back to her bedroom to call Kathleen, and make certain she sold to a family with children—a happy family.

Before she could reach the receiver, the phone rang. Marilyn caught it on the second ring.

"Lynnie?"

"Hi, Sondra. You've got to come see the finished product. I can't believe how the summer flew by, but you were right. Max did a great job. It's like a picture—"

"Is Max there?"

Marilyn sank onto the bed. Sondra's voice sounded husky and upset. "He left a few minutes ago. Why, what's wrong?"

"I've got to find him, Lynnie. He doesn't answer his pager. His crew hasn't seen him all morning."

"Have you tried his house?"

"Answering machine. Oh, Lynnie, Hannibal's been rushed to the hospital." She started to sob. "He fell . . . they think . . . Lynnie, they think he had a stroke."

Marilyn's hand flew to her throat. "Oh, no. Oh, no. Sondra, when? How long ago?"

"I don't know. Mrs. Alford found him. They were

supposed to play bridge this afternoon. He's an early riser, Lynnie. He could have been there for hours."

Marilyn tried to breathe, but barely managed to gasp. "Where's Peter?"

"At the hospital. Lynnie, what am I going to do?"

"You're going to stay calm." She kicked off her heels and reached for her running shoes. "I'll find Max. I promise."

"How?"

She didn't know. He could be anywhere, and she didn't have a car. "I'll find a way. You call Peter, tell him not worry."

"Okay, Lynnie. Hurry."

Marilyn agreed, hung up the phone, and laced up her shoes. Where could he be? *Think, think hard.* He could have gone to the lumberyard, or the hardware store. No, he'd said the jobs were finished. And wouldn't he answer his pager?

She hurried down the steps and across to Mrs. Alford's, then remembered she'd discovered Hannibal and was at the hospital. Marilyn stopped in the middle of the street. Oh, she could use Aunt Phoebe's wisdom right now, but the attic—her escape, her favorite place to think had been cleared out. Her escape—

The elm at his house.

She hurried back inside and called the airlines. "Cancel my flight," she said. "No, I don't want to reschedule. My father, that is, my, oh, someone's sick." Next, she called her office. Her biological father was out, so she left a message on his voice mail. "I'm not coming Monday. Hannibal's in the hospital." She grabbed her purse and started out the door, cell phone in hand. "And I refuse to leave Texas until I know he's okay."

She ran the three blocks to Main Street, and ducked into the first shop she saw—Grandma's Treats.

Petite, white-haired Grandma King, the proprietor, smiled. "Marilyn, I'm so glad you came."

"I need a car," she said. "Hannibal's sick and Max doesn't answer his page. I've got to find him."

Five people held out their keys. Tears filled Marilyn's eyes as she took the nearest set. This is what neighbors did for each other. Why had she resisted it so long?

"I'll keep calling Max's house," Grandma King said.

"Thank you. If you find him before I do, send him to the hospital emergency room."

She climbed into Grandma's rose-emblazoned van and peeled out into traffic. It only took five minutes to reach Max's house, but it felt like an eternity. The tree-lined drive seemed endless and the sun was beginning to set. The Connorses' magnificent antebellum-style home sat on ten acres. If she was going to find him before dark, she had to hurry.

"Max?" she called after jumping out of the truck. No answer. "Max!" she yelled again as she ran up the steps and pounded on the front door. No answer, and no movement from inside—not even any lights on anywhere, so she ran around to the back. "Max, where are you?"

Ten acres of Texas trees and grassland greeted her. Oh, my, she hadn't been here in a long time. What if she didn't find him before Hannibal . . . before he . . . ? Her breath caught and her hands started to shake.

Aunt Phoebe, help me! Somebody, please help me.

The wind whistled past her and suddenly she saw them, a massive tree with limbs that nearly touched the ground and a man hunched underneath, near the massive roots. It had to be him. She threw a thank-you heavenward and dashed toward him. "Max!"

His head snapped up and he stared at her with dark, unforgiving eyes. "What do you want?"

"It's Hannibal," she said, gasping for breath. "Sondra called. He's in the hospital."

Max scrambled to his feet. "Where's Pete?"

"He's already there. Come on, I borrowed Grandma's van. I'll drive you."

"I'll drive."

She took his hand. It shook worse than hers. "No, if I drive I can drop you, then go park. Come on, hurry."

On the way, she related what she knew of Hannibal's accident. Max clutched the door handle with one hand and the dashboard with the other.

"Can't you go faster?" His voice was raw-edged, brimming with near-panic. "Marilyn, floor it!"

"I'm already going ten miles over the limit."

"Just hurry."

Knuckles white from clenching the steering wheel, she did the best she could, but the time—and the miles—dragged by. When they arrived at the hospital, he jumped out almost before she'd stopped and disappeared through the emergency room doors, leaving her alone in the parking lot.

Tears streamed down her face, and she sent up a frantic prayer. "Please, God, watch over Hannibal. Aunt Phoebe . . . Mom. If you've got any pull, use it now. I can't lose the only father I've ever known."

Then she pulled into a parking place and ran to Max's side.

Max strode to the desk, and was met by Pete. "Thank goodness Marilyn found you," he said. "They're running tests now. Looks like, at the very least, he sprained his knee. Fell in the shower. Mrs. Alford found him."

Max turned to the older woman who sat stiffly in the waiting room chair. "Thank you, Mrs. Alford. You okay?"

"Stubborn old fool," she croaked. Her hair stuck up in back and she twisted her hands in her lap. "Why can't he wise up, and get one of those stools for the shower? No shame in being safe."

Max recognized the concern behind her words and squeezed her hand. "Why don't you tell him that when he gets back home?"

She brightened a bit. "Don't think I won't."

"Max, we've got to talk," Pete said, dragging him to a quiet corner. "Pop may need long-term care, a place where someone will check on him regularly."

"He'll be all right," Max insisted, but fear clenched his stomach. Pete was right. Who knew how a stroke might affect their father?

"I hope so, big brother," Pete said. "He's stubborn enough, that's for certain."

"Max?"

He turned as Marilyn approached. She had tear tracks on her face and damp spots on her blouse. "Any news?" she asked.

He shook his head. "Thanks for finding me."

"Yes, thanks, Marilyn," Pete said. "Now that you're here, I'll call Sondra and fill her in."

"Yes, do. She was very upset," Marilyn said. "Oh, and please call Grandma King. I borrowed her van."

"Will do."

Pete walked toward the phones and Max slumped against the wall. What was taking so long?

"Mrs. Alford?" Marilyn said. "You all right?"

"I can't stand this waiting."

"Amen to that," Max said. He couldn't keep his eyes

off the double doors marked NO ADMITTANCE. The rest of the emergency room, the nurses' station, the registration desk, and waiting area faded into a huge void. Nothing remained but those huge green-steel, windowless, double doors.

He started to pace.

"Would you like someone to take you home?" Marilyn asked Mrs. Alford.

"No," the older woman said. "I know I'm not family, but I'd go stir crazy at home."

"You stay right where you are then," Max said.

"Thanks."

He tore his gaze from the doors long enough to glance at the clock. One minute had ticked by. *One* minute! What was taking so long? He paced again. Marilyn fell into step with him.

"How about some coffee and something to eat?" she asked.

"No food. Coffee, okay."

She left, returned in what seemed like hours, and pressed the first of many insulated cups in his hand. Again, she paced along side him. Eventually the hands on the clock began to move. With each passing hour, Max's fear deepened. He told himself they were backed up, that Saturday was a busy night in the emergency room. The delay definitely did *not* mean his father was seriously ill, or incapacitated.

At about 3:00 in the morning, Pete took Mrs. Alford home then came back to stand guard. Sondra called him every hour on his cell phone, but nothing happened. No one came out to talk to them. No one said a word.

"Max?" Marilyn whispered hoarsely at about 5:00. "Do they have a chapel in this hospital?"

"Down the hall."

"I'll be right back."

She left his side and he hugged himself. Without her nearby, chills covered him and hollow fear etched his gut. Pete sat, drumming his fingers on a padded chair, the noise barely audible, but each beat thumped in Max's heart.

Marilyn returned, checked with the nurse on duty, then joined him again. "Nothing yet," she said.

About an hour after sunrise the double doors burst open. Dr. Allan Randalls approached. "Max, Peter, it's good news."

Max halted. "Yeah?"

"Hannibal's knee is a wreck. He claims he fell off a ladder years ago."

"I remember," Max said. "I was still in college."

Allan nodded. "Apparently the bone and cartilage have scraped each other until his knee couldn't support his weight anymore. He bumped his head on the tile when he fell, which is why it took us so long to examine him. We wanted to make certain this accident wasn't caused by . . . anything else."

"Then it wasn't a stroke?" Max held his breath, and every sound ceased—except the pounding of his heart.

"Absolutely not. I'm admitting him, though. He has a pretty big lump on his head, and that knee needs rest and eventual surgery. But we can discuss that after he's recovered."

Relief washed through him and Max let out a long breath. Pop was okay. He wasn't going to die or be a vegetable or any of the hundred other horrible things Max had worried about. He reached up to shake Allan's hand and discovered another one already there. Marilyn's. He'd been gripping it and hadn't even noticed.

Loath to let go of her, he nodded instead. "Thanks, Allan," he said. "Thanks a lot."

Pete sighed and clapped the man on the back. "Yes, thank you very much. Can we see Pop yet?"

"For a few minutes. But not too long. He's had enough excitement for one day."

Pete hurried through the door, and Max stood to follow. Marilyn didn't move. "Aren't you coming?" he asked.

"I'm not a relative." Tears shimmered in her eyes until they shone almost silver. "You go, then tell me how he looks."

"Not a chance," he said. "You're coming with me."

She smiled so big his heart thudded to a stop. They walked hand-in-hand to see Hannibal, and after Max was certain his father would truly be okay, realization began to dawn on him.

"Hey," he said to Marilyn as they walked back through the waiting area, "you're leaving today. You'd better hurry or you'll miss your flight and everything."

She halted, clamped her hands on her hips and glared at him. "Max Connors, you take that back."

"What? What did I say?"

"I'm not leaving with Hannibal in the hospital. What kind of person do you think I am?"

He blinked. "I just thought . . ."

"Well, you thought wrong. I canceled my flight. Family is more important any job."

He kissed her. Right there in front of Pete, the emergency room staff, and everyone else who waited, he drew her into his arms and planted a big one square on her mouth. She melted against him and he knew. He knew she meant to stay. She'd said the magic words—family is more important than any job. He also knew he wanted to marry her. He wanted to celebrate life with her, to hold her in his arms and never let go.

But he couldn't propose here, not in the hospital. "Marilyn," he said, after he broke the kiss, "we need to talk. Alone. In private."

"Where?" she whispered.

"Let's go to your house."

"And let's hurry."

The instant they crossed the threshold of Aunt Phoebe's house, Max pulled Marilyn close. His arms clamped like irons around her body, as though her were afraid she'd get away.

"I'm so glad you stayed," he said hoarsely. "I wanted to ask you, to beg you, not to go back to Chicago."

Her heart skipped a beat. "You did?"

"So much I couldn't sleep nights thinking about it, worrying about how to put my feelings into words."

He halted, glanced around the small foyer, then pulled her away from the door and into her favorite room, the kitchen. Emotion lit his eyes like stars in the night sky. She clung to him, half hoping, half afraid. "Just say it, Max. We're friends, remember?"

"I love you, Marilyn," he said, stroking her cheek. "I love you so much, I don't ever want to let you go."

"Then don't." She kissed him and a dreamy mist surrounded her mind. Could he really love her? After all this time of being alone, had she found someone to share her life? She slid her hands into his hair, threading the thick strands through her fingers. "Don't ever let me go, Max. Ever."

The doorbell rang.

"Ignore it," he said. "Please, ignore it."

"Mmm, maybe they'll go away."

The door opened and a feminine voice called from the foyer. "Marilyn? I know I'm early, but I have some clients from out-of-town who want to see the house."

Marilyn scrambled out of Max's hold, nearly pushing him over. "It's Kathleen! Quick, go out the back. No, wait. Hide."

He arched an eyebrow. "Hide?"

Cupping her hands around her mouth, she yelled out, "Just a minute, Kathleen. Please, just give me a minute and I'll be right there." Heat flushed her cheeks and she clamped her hands on her face. "I know I'm blushing. My cheeks are as hot as firecrackers. I'm just not used to this."

"This?"

She lowered her voice to the barest whisper. "I feel like a teenager caught necking behind the school gym."

"Exciting, huh?" He stroked her cheek and grinned.

She paused, then grinned back. "Yeah, it is."

"Marilyn?" Kathleen called again.

"I'll get rid of her," Marilyn promised, then hurried out of the kitchen and met Kathleen at the front door.

"Good morning," Marilyn said. "Sorry to keep you waiting." Her heart fluttered with happiness. "There's been a change."

"You're going to bake for Grandma's Treats after all?"

Marilyn blinked. "What?"

"I saw the van outside—Grandma's Treats. I thought maybe you'd changed your mind."

"Well, no, I—"

"Good." Kathleen started to the front door. "Then I'll get my clients."

"You mean they're here now, waiting?" Marilyn

cleared her throat. "I wish I'd known. I mean, I'm sorry, but . . ."

Some dishes rattled and the scent of cinnamon wafted on the air. "Marilyn?" Max called. "Honey, you want coffee?"

She looked over her shoulder. He poked his head out of the kitchen and smiled. Her breath caught. Greek god was an understatement.

"Yes, please, but give me a moment. I'm explaining—"

"No explanations necessary," Kathleen said, admiration oozing from her voice. She laid a hand on Marilyn's arm and whispered, "For that, I'd hang around, too." Then she left.

Marilyn turned to run into the kitchen, back into his arms, but the doorbell rang again. This time it was Grandma King and several of the neighbors.

"We heard about Hannibal," she said. "How is he?"

"He'll be all right," Marilyn said, straining to keep the disappointment out of her voice. "Please, come in, won't you?"

Max strode up behind her. "Come in, everyone," he said. "Have some coffee. I just made a fresh pot."

The neighbors pushed past her, oohing and aahing at the restoration, and Marilyn grimaced. She wanted to be with Max, to confess her feelings, to discuss their future. He drew her out onto the back porch, out of sight of the others, and kissed her.

"These people are liable to stay for hours," he said. "Thought I'd better kiss you now while I still had the chance."

"I like the way you think." She laid her head on his shoulder. "But we didn't get a chance to finish our talk."

"Looks like that'll have to wait for now."

"But not for long?"

He kissed the top of her head. "I hope not. We Greek gods are short on patience."

"Then meet me here tonight, on the back porch like before."

He hugged her. "It's a date."

Chapter Ten

The next morning, Monday, Marilyn hopped out of bed at sunrise. She threw open the window, and took a good look at her new hometown. Cool, sweet air filled her lungs, birds chirped, and people waved as they walked down the street.

Max had been unable to return the night before, but she hadn't minded—too much. All day, neighbors and friends had stopped by to get news of Hannibal, and to welcome her home.

They'd said that, too. "Welcome home, Marilyn."

Mrs. Alford, who'd insisted Marilyn call her Betty, had visited in the evening, complaining she'd now have competition at the bake-off next year. Marilyn had assured her they were a team. Together, they'd take all comers. Betty had left with a smile on her face, and a couple of new recipes in her purse.

Today, Marilyn had an appointment to talk with Grandma King about becoming a baker for the little café. She'd probably have to upgrade her kitchen for the license, and maybe make other changes as well, which was why she'd risen so early. She wanted to get a head start on her new life.

A life that included Max.

Max called later that afternoon. "I've got to meet with homeowners tonight, honey," he said. "Then I'm going to the hospital to see Pop. Wanna come?"

"Yes," she said breathlessly. She loved being called "honey." It made her feel like she belonged, like she was special. "Can you come get me? I'm without transportation."

"Pick you up at eight, and don't be late."

She smiled, hung up the phone, then busied herself unpacking her suitcase—for good—and reading a library book on commercial baking. The librarian, who'd been so helpful with the restoration of her aunt's antiques, had also given her the name and phone number of the licensing board. Tomorrow, she'd start down that route. When she had an idea of what needed to be done to upgrade the kitchen, she'd talk to Max.

He met her that night, full of energy. After a too-quick kiss, he launched into a spiel about an old funeral home out on the farm-to-market road.

"Max, slow down," she said.

"I'm driving the speed limit."

She laughed lightly. "No, I mean you're talking so fast I can't understand what you're saying."

"They want me to restore it. The whole thing. Honey, it's twice the size of your house."

Her chest expanded with pride. "Max, that's wonderful. But what about the other restorations you mentioned?"

"Not a problem. Those people want to wait until spring, so as to not interfere with the holidays." He paused. "It's September. I can't believe the end of the year is almost here."

"Time flies when you're having fun."

"Yeah." He stopped the truck and pulled her across the seat. "Speaking of fun, is your back porch booked for tonight?"

She sighed. "I have one standing reservation. Max Connors. If he doesn't show, then maybe I can work you in."

He kissed her nose, then started up the truck again. "You're a nut, but I like that in a woman."

"Good, because what you see is what you get."

He waggled his eyebrows. "Hmmm, I like the sound of that."

They reached the hospital and quickly spoke with Hannibal. Peter and Sondra were there, with the children, crowding the small room. The nurse eventually pushed them out and Peter, with baby Peter in his arms, drew Max aside.

"So," Sondra whispered to Marilyn, holding Emily and Joseph with each hand, "rumor has it you're sticking around."

Marilyn glanced at Max then blushed. "Well, yes."

"Then kindly tell me why I had to hear it from my next-door neighbor? What's the matter? You can't pick up a phone?"

"Hear what, Mommy?" Joseph asked.

"Aunt Marilyn's going to stay a while longer, and live in the big house Uncle Max was working on," Sondra said.

He clapped. "Goody. She's fun."

Emily imitated her older brother. "Aunt Mar'win fun."

Warmth spread through Marilyn's entire body. They liked her and they thought she was *fun*. She knelt in front of Joseph. "I think you're fun, too."

"And me?" Emily asked, tugging on Marilyn's arm.

"You, too," she said and glanced up at Sondra. "May I baby-sit sometime?"

Sondra laughed. "Are you kidding? What mother wouldn't want a baby-sitter her children adore? Of course you can."

"What's this?" Max asked. "Am I being pushed out of a job?"

Both children hugged his legs tightly. "Aunt Marilyn's going to live in that big house, Uncle Max," Joseph said.

Max glanced up at her, his eyes full of affection and questions. "She is?" he asked. "Aunt Marilyn?"

"It's an honorary title," she said quickly.

"Well," he said, "we'll just have to do something to change that, won't we?"

She frowned. What did that mean?

Sondra winked. "Come to supper Saturday," she said. "We'll celebrate Pop's homecoming and . . . everything."

Max put an arm around Marilyn's shoulders. "That okay with you, honey?"

"Yes." When he called her honey, everything was A-okay.

"Great." Sondra and the kids joined Peter and walked away.

Max turned Marilyn into his arms, then kissed her nose. "I have to stand you up tonight."

"Why?"

"Believe it or not, the Fergusons made yet another change."

"I've never met them," she said, frowning, "but I'm convinced they're the most indecisive people on the planet."

"Yeah, I was pretty steamed up, too, until they explained."

She gazed into his eyes, and saw delight there. Puzzled, she asked, "What possible excuse could they have for changing at this late date?"

"They're having a baby."

Envy rushed through her. "Oh?"

"You should have seen them. They've been a complete pain all along." He took her hand and headed for the exit. "But tonight, they fell all over themselves to please me."

"Because they don't want to pay for the changes?"

"No. Just the opposite. They don't care about the money. Apparently, they've been trying to have children for years and had given up. Now, naturally, they're focused on childproofing and having the nursery near the master bedroom."

"Of course," she said, ashamed of herself for jumping to conclusions. "So you've got some redesigning to do."

"Phone calls to make. Crews to reschedule. Some of my people are seasonal help. Before they go back to their other jobs, I need to see how many of them I can put on this one."

She looped her arm through his. She loved him so much already. Now, he was willing to give up his spare time, probably even his sleep to redo a house for people who'd been troublesome from the beginning. "You're a nice man, Max Connors."

He snorted. "You sure know how to kill a guy's ego."

"Excuse me." She giggled. "You're a benevolent Greek god."

"Better."

He drove her home and kissed her goodnight under the porch light, in front of the entire neighborhood. Mrs. Alford opened her door and waved. Two other neighbors applauded. Marilyn should have been embarrassed, but she wasn't. She loved it. People cared and they showed it. No matter what happened between her and Max, she'd never ignore her neighbors again. Having them as friends felt too good to let the opportunity pass by.

To prove her loyalty, tomorrow she'd put her plan into action. Then she could remain a Connorsville neighbor as long as they'd have her.

By Saturday, Max was as frustrated as a bent nail. He hadn't been alone with Marilyn since he'd kissed her good night on Monday. He'd talked to her on the phone, seen her at the hospital visiting Hannibal, but their back porch rendezvous had been postponed—again.

Restoring her house had definitely turned the tide for Connors and Son. Calls for work came in so often, he'd hired someone just to answer the phone. The Fergusons settled on their changes, and he'd managed to rehire his seasonal crew. Plus, Kathleen Griffith had connected him with the couple who'd wanted to buy Marilyn's house. They were bidding on another one like it, and wanted Max to restore it from top to bottom.

Ironically, when he longed for spare time—time to spend with Marilyn—he had more work than he could handle.

Tonight, though, he'd see her at Pete's, and no matter what happened he intended to get her alone and propose. He wasn't going to lose any more time, or let her think about leaving. He was going to pop the question and hope she could transfer her job to Connorsville, or Dallas. He couldn't let her get away.

He picked her up at seven. She wore her hair up, and a simple strand of pearls circled her swanlike neck. Her sky-blue dress deepened the gray of her eyes.

"You look wonderful," he said.

She smiled. "Thank you. So do you."

"Thanks." He tugged at his collar. Sondra had insisted they dress up, so he'd donned a suit and tie. "But I'm choking to death."

"Oh, too bad." She looped her arm through his. "Because I think you look exceptionally Greek god-ish this evening."

"Thanks." He bowed slightly, patting his pocket, and the jeweler's box within. He couldn't wait to get through tonight's celebration so he could beg Marilyn to be his Greek goddess.

Pop greeted them at Pete's front door, looking healthy and happy. "Marilyn Waters, you're as pretty as—"

"New-poured concrete?" she said with a laugh.

"Nah, more like an angel in a Christmas pageant."

"Oh, Hannibal, you're sweet."

"I told you to call me Pop," he insisted. He eyed Max suspiciously. "Who's this guy?"

Marilyn giggled. "Pop, it's Max."

He gave her a look of mock horror. "Great Scott, he's wearing a suit. What are you folks trying to do, scare the rest of the life out of me?" He grabbed Max in a huge bear hug, and whispered, "You happy, son?"

"You bet, Pop." Max released his father, then drew Marilyn close. "Everything seems to be working out just fine."

"Good," Hannibal said. "Let's get this show on the road."

"What's your hurry?" Max asked.

"I'm going over to Betty's later."

Sondra sighed. "I tried to get her to come to supper tonight, but she insisted on not intruding on family time."

"You couldn't talk her into it, Pop?" Max said. "After all, we owe her one. She saved your skin."

"She's a stubborn old woman."

"She cares about you," Marilyn said softly.

Pop reddened. "Yeah, well, that goes both ways."

"Sounds like you're pretty happy, too," Max said.

"Dang it, stop yakking and let's eat." Pop tried to look serious, but Max saw the sparkle in the older man's eyes. Marilyn was right. Betty was sweet on Hannibal, and the feeling was apparently mutual. Good. His father deserved it. Besides, Max wanted everyone to feel as good as he did.

They adjourned to the dining room where they ate a delicious meal on heirloom china. The tablecloth was Irish linen from Sondra's family, and the crystal had been a gift from Max's great-grandpa to his new bride. Everything spoke of tradition and family. Max couldn't remember feeling so content.

After Pete's kids had been put to bed, the five adults sat around the table chatting. Max stood and raised his glass of sparkling cider. "I propose a toast. To Pop's recovery, and his future as the best scrounger in the construction business."

Marilyn, who sat on his right, leaped to her feet. "To Pop."

Hannibal stood and squared his shoulders. "To Max, the best carpenter this side of anywhere, and to Marilyn, who's finally come home where she belongs."

"Right where she belongs," Max said softly. He turned

to her, looped his arm through hers and drank from his glass—wedding-toast style—then kissed her.

"Now we're cooking with gas," Pop said.

Sondra, Pete, and Pop applauded, but Max kept his gaze focused on Marilyn's face. Did she get the message? When he proposed later—on one knee—would she be surprised?

She blushed then cleared her throat. "How about dessert?"

"Think Max already had his," Pop said, laughing loudly.

"Did you bake something special?" Max whispered.

"Yes, a surprise," she said and scurried into the kitchen.

When she returned Max's jaw dropped. Surprise was a woeful understatement. Marilyn had "built" a layer cake in the shape of Aunt Phoebe's Victorian farmhouse—right down to the gingerbread trim and the stained-glass front door.

He'd never seen anything like it. "Honey, you are a marvel."

"Marvel, nothing," Hannibal proclaimed, "she's an artist. "Do they give out master's licenses to bakers?"

"This goes beyond cookies and pastry," Pete added. "You've created a masterpiece here."

"Wait. Don't anyone cut it," Sondra insisted. "I'm going to get my camera and take a picture."

Marilyn gazed up at him. "Do you really think it's okay?"

"Okay? It's incredible." Max put an arm around her shoulders. "Pop's right. You're an artist."

"Thank you," she said quietly, then snuggled closer. "Can I talk to you about it more, later?"

"You bet."

"Okay, everyone," Sondra said, "line up and smile." After she took innumerable shots, from innumerable angles, she added, "Now, let's have coffee in the family room."

"Isn't Pop going to cut the cake?" Marilyn asked, her eyes wide.

"Darlin', I build houses, not tear 'em down."

"But—"

"Lynnie, no way are we ruining what had to be hours of work." Sondra put the cake back in the kitchen and brought out a silver tray laden with cookies.

"I didn't bake it to look good," Marilyn insisted. "I made it to eat."

"I'll take a piece later." Max leaned down and whispered, "Save me the back porch."

She blushed. "Always."

"If you two are through making goo-goo eyes at each other," Pop said, "I want to talk to Marilyn."

Max reluctantly let her go, and she moved to perch on the ottoman near Hannibal's favorite chair. She leaned forward to talk, and Max couldn't help but make "goo-goo" eyes at her. Her face glowed with excitement. She looked so perfect sitting there, like one of the family. Then she shivered.

He moved behind her, draped his jacket over her shoulders and let his hands rest there.

"Can't let her out of reach, huh, Max?" Pop asked.

"She looked cold," Max said, aware his family was watching him like a hawk.

"Thank you," Marilyn said. "I was, a little."

"Hmmmm." Sondra winked. "What a husband-like thing to do."

The jeweler's box practically burned a hole in Max's pocket, but he couldn't say anything. Not yet. Not until he'd spoken to Marilyn. She gazed up at him, her eyes bright with what he hoped was love. He squeezed her shoulder and smiled.

"Well, come on, Max, tell us," Sondra said. "Are we about to hear the chime of wedding bells?"

"Sondra!" Marilyn said, blushing.

" 'Bout time," Hannibal muttered.

"Pop!" Marilyn blushed deeper.

"And the pitter-patter of little feet," Pete added.

"Pitter-patter?" Marilyn's blush faded.

"Now that you mention it," Max said, looking at Marilyn. "I have been thinking about the next generation of Connors and Son a lot lately. A boy, a son of my own to teach carpentry and home building. Someone to pass down Great-Grandpa's skills."

"Don't be so provincial, Max," Sondra insisted. "You could teach a daughter just the same."

"Girls shouldn't wield a hammer," Hannibal snapped.

"Pop, join the twenty-first century," Pete said. "As long as she's raven-haired with midnight eyes, you'd be just a happy with a granddaughter to spoil."

"But, Peter," Marilyn said, her voice small, "you have sandy hair and blue eyes."

"I'm the middle child," Pete said.

"It's tradition, darlin'," Hannibal said. "Not only does the business go from eldest son to eldest son, they all look alike, too."

"Talk about obvious heredity," Sondra said. "From great-grandfather down, the eldest sons all look like Max and Pop."

"*Exactly* like Max?" Marilyn asked, her voice breaking.

She went rigid beneath his fingers, like concrete setting up on a hot day. He frowned. "Honey—"

"I'd like to go home, please." She pulled away from him.

Hannibal leaned toward her. "You okay, darlin'?"

"I have a headache," she said, "and it's getting worse by the minute. Please, Max."

"Sure." He held out his hand, but she didn't take it. Concern gripped him. Her skin was ashen and her eyes were bloodshot. "Marilyn, you look awful."

"I'll be all right," she said, giving him a wide berth. "Let's just go home."

He smiled inwardly. She'd said "let's go home." Maybe this was a ruse to get them alone. But why so dramatic? He didn't have any secrets from his family. Why not just tell them they wanted to go home and neck? Heck, Pop would probably order up a police escort to hurry them along.

Once they were alone, Max tried to draw her closer, but she hurried into his truck. He frowned and wondered if he'd said something wrong. As soon as they pulled up to her house, he tried again. "Marilyn, I have something very important I want to discuss."

"Me, too," she said. She removed his jacket and laid on the seat between them. "If you don't mind, I'll go first."

He swallowed. "Go ahead."

"I'm flying home to Chicago tomorrow."

His heart stopped beating and he sucked air, but nothing filled his lungs. "What? Why?"

"It's time."

"No. You said you were going to stay." He reached for her and she pulled back again. "Tell me what's wrong."

"I'm under a lot of stress. I told you I didn't lose my

job, but if I don't go back, I will. Then all my plans will go down the drain."

"Marilyn, I love you. I don't want you to go."

"I have to," she said, firmly. "RSW is downsizing. Dozens of people will be scrambling to find jobs before Christmas. I can help them and myself at the same time." She stared at her hands. "I can't abandon those people at holiday time."

"Of course not, but that doesn't have to be the end of it. Go to Chicago, fix the problem, and come back."

"It could take months."

"So, it could take months. I'm not going anywhere."

"Max, please."

"Please, what? What aren't you telling me?"

"Nothing," she said, turning to face him. "It's just time to say good-bye."

Clouds darkened her gray eyes as certainly as a spring thunderstorm. Max began to get worried. "Goodbye?" he said, his voice ragged and broken. "I don't believe it."

"Fine, Max. Have it your way."

"*My* way is for you to live in Texas. For us to live in Texas."

"That's the problem, we're headed in different directions. We always have been."

"But I thought we worked that out, or were about to. What happened?"

"I'm just following the terms of our original agreement. No ties, no commitments."

His heart thumped. "Are you saying you don't love me?"

Silence. Max held his breath waiting for her answer. If she left, he'd lose his structure, his support. Without her, he'd crumble like a house without a foundation.

"Love isn't the issue, Max," she said, her voice flat and distant. "Never has been."

Not the issue?

He flinched. No. This couldn't be happening. Not again. Marilyn wasn't another Brittany, she couldn't be leaving him for her job. "Are you sorry we became friends—more than friends?"

"Oh no. This summer's been wonderful. A dream come true."

Hopeful, he reached for her. She jerked out of his grasp.

"So why leave?" he asked, his voice gruff.

"Because the alarm went off."

"What alarm? What are you talking about?"

"Dream's over, Max. Time for me to wake up and rejoin the real world."

"Real world?" Max's head spun. Was she saying that Texas wasn't real, or what they felt for each other wasn't real? "Marilyn, I don't understand. Let's talk about this."

"I can't. I mean, there's nothing to talk about. It was wonderful. I loved it. I loved you, but love isn't the issue."

She reached for the door handle, but he managed to stall her—just. "Then what *is* the issue?"

"Please, don't make me say it, Max. Please just let me go."

"Say what? Marilyn, tell me what's wrong and I'll fix it."

"Not even you can fix this. I . . . I" Her voice caught and she swallowed, pain etching lines along her mouth. "Max, I can't have children. I can't give you raven-haired babies or any babies."

"What?" Beyond stunned, Max felt himself frown and

saw her reaction—the pain lines around her mouth deepened.

"Let me go," she pleaded.

"Wait. Is that the issue?" he asked, trying to stall so he could think. "Because if it is, it isn't. I mean, it doesn't matter."

Her gray eyes clouded further and she scowled at him. "Max, don't lie to me. I heard you tonight. It does matter, it matters a lot. I can see it in your face right now."

"That's just surprise," he said shakily. "Really."

"It's disappointment, and you know it. But that's okay, because you'll make a great father. You *should* complete tradition and hand down your expertise to your own son—you should achieve your dreams. Please, Max, just let me go. I know all about broken dreams and I couldn't bear to break yours."

Before he could say another word, she got out of the car and walked away.

Chapter Eleven

Frozen by disbelief, Max sat like a statue, clenching the steering wheel, his mind reeling.

"I can't have children."

In a million years, he never would have guessed that was her secret. Not in a trillion years. When he'd imagined them together, he'd assumed they'd fill the homestead with lots of children. Ache settled around his heart. Of course he was disappointed. Not only about the news, but the fact she hadn't trusted him with the truth. Weren't they friends?

If not, what had they been doing all summer? Playing? He couldn't think. Nothing made sense. So many ideas, plans, and dreams swirled in his head, all out of reach now. Glancing up at her house, he knew he'd never solve anything sitting here, so he started the truck and headed for home and bed. But sleep eluded him. He paced. He showered. He paced some more, but no matter what he did, Marilyn's last words ran through his mind. Over and over and over.

"I know all about broken dreams and I couldn't bear to break yours."

His dream. Her dream. They'd talked about everything else, but the future. Why hadn't they talked it over? Friends would have discussed it, sorted it, worked through it, but they hadn't. Why? Had he been so hurt by Brittany that he couldn't trust another woman with his feelings? Did Marilyn feel she couldn't trust him?

Frustrated, he worked through the questions all night, retreating to Great-Grandpa's elm, hoping for some insight from beyond. When the sun rose, he still didn't have an answer and trudged back to the homestead—to discover the phone ringing.

Hoping it was Marilyn, he snatched it up. "Hello?"

"Well? Come on, son, spill it. What's the date?"

"Pop?" Max slumped onto the kitchen chair and stared at the clock. 6:30. "Pop, what are you talking about?"

"You and Marilyn. You proposed, didn't you? Hell's bells, son, it was written all over your face last night. When's the wedding? Think her stuffy old father will come?"

Heartache clamped Max. He had been obvious. Now he had to endure the explanations. "I didn't ask her."

"What? Why not?"

"I didn't get a chance. She's going back to Chicago."

"Are you kidding? What in the blue blazes for?"

Max blew out a breath. "She can't have children, Pop."

"No?" Hannibal sighed deeply. "Ah, poor darling, and we went on and on about tradition. If I didn't have a bum knee I'd kick myself."

"Yeah, me, too."

"You deserve it. Can't believe I raised such a talented but idiotic son."

"What?" Max arched an eyebrow. "What are you talking about?"

"You love her, don't you?"

"Very much."

"And you let her get away."

"Pop, I tried to stop her, but she wouldn't listen."

Hannibal muttered something Max couldn't quite catch, then blurted out. "Do you care whether she can have kids?"

"Yes. No." He sat suddenly, surprised to find he didn't care. Yeah, he was disappointed, but which would be worse? To be without children? Or without Marilyn? "I am a prize fool."

"Not if you go after her you aren't."

"On my way. Thanks, Pop. Call you later."

"Just bring her home where she belongs."

Max grabbed his keys and headed for Marilyn's house, but when he got there, no one was home. Instead, a note was taped to the stained glass, a note in Marilyn's handwriting—to Sondra. Even though he knew he shouldn't, he read it.

Forgive me for being a coward and taking an earlier flight, but I couldn't face telling everyone goodbye. Believe me, it's better this way.

Love,
Marilyn

"No, it isn't better this way," he said, crumpling the note. "Not better for me. Not better for you, and definitely not better for us."

Determined to catch up with her and convince her of it, he climbed into his pickup and sped toward the airport.

Marilyn gazed out the airplane window, watching Dallas recede behind her. After a sleepless night, she'd packed and fled Texas on the first flight out of Dallas–Fort Worth. Tears threatened to spill over, but she couldn't fault her behavior. No, she'd done nothing wrong. In fact, she'd done Max a favor.

She'd saved him from marrying a flawed woman.

How could she have let herself forget Connors tradition? Had love blinded her to the facts? No way on earth would she ever bear Max's child, raven-haired or otherwise. A hundred years of Connors history stood behind him, and she refused to be the one to tear it down.

He'd reacted just as she'd expected, covering his disappointment and claiming he didn't care. He was that good and that honorable—like the benevolent Greek god she'd teased him about being. Gerald had reacted the same way, at first. But she knew better. Men cared about stuff like that, about passing on their genes to a new generation and leaving a little something of themselves behind. Oh, yes, Gerald had promised he didn't care, but the night before their wedding he'd sat her down and not-too-gently declared he could never marry a woman who wasn't whole.

So, she'd left. Yes, it hurt. Oh boy, did it hurt, but it was better this way. Not only to save herself more anguish, but because Max deserved to have his dream, all of it. She'd get over the pain.

In about a million years.

Which is about how long the flight took. Thunderstorms delayed their takeoff and slowed their travel time.

By the time she reached Chicago, she was over two hours late. Storm clouds darkened the skyline, and dreary rain plopped onto to the concrete. Exhausted and sad beyond belief, she trudged to her one bedroom apartment and sagged onto the contemporary sofa, dropping her suitcases at her feet.

Still wrapped in her raincoat, she curled into a ball, hugging herself. Sunset filtered through the storm and the hours ticked by, but she didn't move. Food didn't interest her. Unpacking held no meaning. Nothing meant anything without Max, not even starting her own business. Her head pounded and her heart thudded dully.

As she lay there in her darkened apartment, lightning split the late afternoon sky. She automatically began her count. "One thousand one, one thousand two." Thunder boomed, rattling the sliding glass door to her balcony. "Yes!" she cried. "Let it storm, let the noise block out every single thought." Even if bad news followed, what could hurt worse than leaving the man she loved?

A peculiar knocking interrupted her thoughts and she sat up. Was someone at her door? She ignored it. She didn't want to see anyone. Besides, she didn't know any of her neighbors, so it must be a salesman, or someone who had the wrong apartment.

"Marilyn?" a deep voice called. "Are you in there?"

Max? On shaky legs she crossed the inexpensive beige carpet to peer through the peephole. A familiar male figure shadowed her door. Max came after her? Didn't he understand it was over?

"Marilyn, please," he said, and knocked again, harder.

After a deep sigh, she opened the door and motioned him inside. Hoping to lighten the tension, she repeated her words from that stormy meeting at the beginning of summer. "Hello, Max. Nice day, isn't it?"

"For fish, maybe," he answered, following along.

She motioned him inside, but he halted just over the threshold. The dimly lit hallway and darkened apartment surrounded them like a warm blanket. Her heart skipped a beat, and she drank in the sight of him. The rain had flattened his silky mane to his head and darkened his denim shirt. He looked as though he'd been tossed into a swimming pool, but to Marilyn, he was the most beautiful sight she'd ever seen.

"I thought we'd said our good-byes," she said, getting him a towel to dry off.

"You did," he said, his voice rough. "I didn't."

"I don't understand," she said, shutting the door and leaning against it for support. "We knew from the beginning this wouldn't be permanent."

"That's what we said."

"Then why are you here?"

"To bring you home," he said, reaching for her.

"I am home." Ducking out of his reach, she moved across the room to stare out the patio door. Her throat constricted, and her voice scraped like sandpaper. "So, please, just go back to Connorsville and forget this summer ever happened."

He came up behind her, close enough for her to feel his body heat. More than anything she wished she could lean into his embrace and rely on his strength. But she didn't dare.

"I don't want to forget," he said.

"I do."

He sucked in air, and she knew she'd hurt him, but she had no choice. She had to get him out of her life for good—for his good.

"I know what you're doing," he said quietly. "You're

Built to Last

being deliberately mean to force me to go home. But I'm not leaving, not until we've talked this out."

"No!" She faced him. "There's no point. No matter what you say, you and I will never work. You might think so right now, but in the end you'll wind up resenting me."

"Marilyn, I'd never resent you. I love you and having children isn't that import—"

"No," she said, putting a finger to his lips. "No, Max. Don't make any sacrifices for me. I'm not worth it."

"Not worth it?" Concern softened his gaze. "What . . . idiot told you that?"

"Gerald."

"Who in the world is Gerald?"

"My ex-fiancé."

His eyebrows shot up. "You were engaged?"

"Two years ago. He claimed it didn't matter, either, but he left me for another, more complete woman."

"Ouch, that must have hurt."

Marilyn gulped air and faced the patio door again. "You have no idea."

"I think I do," he said, and blew out a long breath. "I was engaged once, to Brittany, and when she left me, I thought I'd never get over it. And I *knew* I'd never love again. Then you came along."

Tears streamed down her cheeks, imitating the rainwater on the glass. "Max, please don't."

"I have to, Marilyn. We're friends, right? And friends don't keep secrets." He approached her again, his voice rumbling like the echo of distant thunder. "Which is why I have to ask this. Why did you keep this all to yourself?"

"What?" She turned, surprised to no longer see disappointment in his eyes, but sympathy. "What do you mean?"

"I mean this is a big burden to carry all alone. When did you find out?"

"My first gynecological exam," she said, remembering it in depressing detail. "The doctor said that conceiving would be a one-in-a-million shot, and carrying to term would take a miracle."

"And you've kept that a secret all this time?"

"Yes," she said past the lump in her throat. "Sondra doesn't even know."

"Oh, honey," he crooned, and drew her into his arms.

"You have to understand, Max," Marilyn said, giving into the impulse to bury her face in his shirt. "I had to leave you. All that Connors history and tradition, I couldn't ruin that for you. And I couldn't ruin the one place I've always been happy. Does that make any sense?"

"You mean you didn't want the dream to end?"

"Yes."

"So even if I say I don't care about having children, you still won't believe me?"

"It's not a matter of belief, Max. It's about you staying where you belong and having what you deserve."

"Well, do I deserve to be happy?"

"Of course. Absolutely."

"Then you shouldn't have left."

She leaned back to gaze into his face. "But Max—"

"Marilyn, listen to me," he said, cupping her face. "Yeah, I want children." Her heart broke and she struggled to get out of his hold until he added, "But I want you more."

She gasped. "You do?"

"When I found out you'd left, I crumpled, like someone had snatched the earth right out from under my feet. I'm incomplete without you, Marilyn. Lost and alone. I don't need a mirror-image son or daughter to make me happy, but I do need you. Don't leave me without a foundation, honey. Please."

Afraid to believe, she searched his face, like the morning they'd rushed to her house after Hannibal's recovery; love lit Max's eyes like stars in the night sky. *Oh, boy.* Here's what she'd dreamed about for so long: of belonging, of loving someone and being loved back. She could have it all—*if* she had the courage to put aside her fears. Could she?

She searched within, and in moments the answer leaped from her heart into her mind. *Yes, yes, oh, yes!*

"I'll never leave you, Max," she murmured. "I promise."

"Then's there only one thing left to do." He kissed her, and asked, his voice low and deep, "Marilyn, will you marry me?"

Love lightened her heart until she was giddy and she giggled. "Of course I will. How could I say no to a Greek god?"

He pulled back, still cupping her face, and peered into her eyes, his mouth split into a broad smile. "Then you'll be my Greek goddess and away with me to Mount Olympus?"

"Oh, yes," she whispered. "For eternity and beyond."

Epilogue

Four years later

Lightning split the late-afternoon sky. Thunder exploded overhead, rattling the windows of Aunt Phoebe's house. Marilyn gasped, but she didn't start to count. After four years of living with Texas storms, she'd grown accustomed to the noise—and accepted that bad news didn't always follow.

With that in mind, she tried not to think about the phone, about the fact that it should have rung with news long ago.

Instead, she focused on the atmosphere inside. Cinnamon and ginger scented the air. Clanging filled the kitchen. Marilyn turned and smiled. Red-orange light slanted through the window, illuminating the corner where golden-haired Angela Hope Connors banged on Marilyn's best cake pan.

"Sweetie," Marilyn said, "play Mama another song."

Two-year-old Angela gleefully picked up a second wooden spoon and serenaded her mother with all the might her chubby arms could manage. "Mama wike my song?" she asked.

"Mama wuv your song." Marilyn gazed down at the child and sighed. Her daughter. The adoption had gone through over a year ago, but she still had trouble believing she and Max were parents of the most adorable little girl.

The timer buzzed, interrupting her thoughts. "Uh-oh," Angela said. "Uh-oh."

Marilyn reached first for the phone, then realized her mistake and bent to kiss her daughter's golden curls. Angela had already learned the significance of that electronic buzz.

"Time for cookies," Marilyn said, then grabbed a towel and swiped the perspiration from her forehead. The Texas summer had dragged on and on and on. She hoped the storm would bring the relief of cooler temperatures. "Otherwise, sweetie," she said to Angela, "you'll have to go trick-or-treat in your swimsuit."

She placed a tray of rolls in one oven, and a sheet of gingersnaps in a second, and a deep male voice said, "Swimming? Don't think we'll have *that* much rain."

"Max!" Marilyn turned and opened her arms to her Greek god of a husband. "Hi! We didn't expect you so soon."

"Storm forced us to finish early." He drew her close and whispered in her ear, "Thought my girl might be a bit skittish."

"Me?" she asked, laying her head on his shoulder. "Nah."

"Good, because if you're about finished—"

"Dada!" Angela scrambled to her feet and reached for him. "Dada carry me!"

He swooped her into his arms, twirled her, then placed her on his shoulders. Marilyn laughed and glanced with pride at Aunt Phoebe's house. With Grandma King as a partner, she had turned it into a Victorian-style teahouse—showcasing her desserts.

"Hey, Mama," Max said, his grin broad and bright, "when's Marilyn's Marvels going to close?"

She grabbed an apple turnover and popped it into his mouth. "I just have one batch left and they're baking now."

"Me, too, Mama," Angela said, clapping her hands.

Marilyn broke off a small bit of pastry and put it on her daughter's tongue. "There you go, sweetie. Chew carefully."

Max kissed her. How he managed it with Angela on his shoulders, Marilyn couldn't imagine, but he planted a smacking kiss right on her lips. "Mmm, Mama tastes good today."

"I feel good," she said. "Better than I've felt in my entire life."

He dragged his gaze over her shorts and T-shirt–clad body then winked. "You look good, too."

"Thank you." She was a sweaty mess, but she didn't argue. "You're the best husband ever."

He grinned. "Best daddy, too?"

"Best daddy, too."

He grinned broader and started dancing down the hall, Angela still on his shoulders. Marilyn finished up with the last of the baking, picked up Angela's "musical instruments," and loaded the dishwasher. Then she ran a hand over the countertop and stared out the window. Brilliant red roses and purple petunias gleamed in the afternoon sun, daring the coming storm to whip off their petals. She smiled. Much had changed since she'd come to Connorsville that summer so many years ago. Yet, the things that mattered—this friendly community, her aunt's house, and her love for Max—had stayed the same.

"I did it, Aunt Phoebe," she said to the air. "I carved my niche in life, and I'm happy, so incredibly happy. I couldn't have done it without this house, without your love. Thank you."

"Mama dance!" Angela shrieked from the front of the house.

"Yeah, Marilyn, come celebrate with us."

Her breath caught and she rushed into the parlor. "Celebrate? Did they call?" Her hand flew to her throat. "Is that why you're here early?"

Max drew Angela off his shoulders and nodded. "The adoption agency caught me just as I was on my way here. They have a baby girl, Marilyn. If you want, we can pick her up today."

"Of course I want." She paused and gazed into her husband's midnight eyes. "But what about you, Max? What about your dream of following tradition, of passing Connors and Son to your son?"

"We'll start a new Connors family tradition," he said, stroking her cheek. "The business and the carpentry skills will pass down from father to *daughter.* I can't wait."

Tears filled her eyes. "Oh, I love you, Max Connors."

"Not half as much as I love you."

The three of them—her family—stood together a long moment. Marilyn hugged them, reluctant to let go.

"So, come on, Mama," Max said, planting a loud smack on his daughter's chubby cheek. "My little angel wants to meet her new baby sister."

Angela clapped and grinned. "Baby. My baby."

Marilyn laughed and sent them outside while she checked the kitchen, turned off the lights and locked up. She could hear Max and Angela giggling, and stopped to watch them roll in the fresh mown grass. Tears welled up, tears of contentment, and she counted her blessings. After years of loneliness and doubts, her dream had become reality and she had everything she could possibly want.

A home, a family, and her greatest dream of all—a love built to last.

SOMERSWORTH PUBLIC LIBRARY
25 MAIN STREET
SOMERSWORTH, NH 03878-3198